FIRE FOR TWO

JILL WEBB

www.sincyrpublishing.com
sincyr.submissions@gmail.com

Novella Published by SinCyr Publishing, University Place, WA 98466
Copyright © 2020

Print ISBN: 978-1-948780-30-8

Edited by Rhiannon Rhys-Jones
Copy edit by Sienna Saint-Cyr
Cover by Lee Moyer

For Nikki and Robyn, the best daughters anyone could have.

CONTENTS

CHAPTER ONE

Iona pushed the flame across her palm. Another mental nudge and it twirled in a lazy circle.

"Now something else," Dr. Choi said, flipping through Iona's chart.

Iona concentrated on the flame until it grew, split into five, and sent each separate flame zipping to a fingertip. She let them dance there for a bit, then put them out one at a time. Just because the exam room was fireproof didn't mean Iona wanted to risk burning up all the oxygen on this level. Basement and sub-basement didn't have the best ventilation, no matter what they said.

The doc just hmmm'ed and tore a sheet of paper from her clipboard and placed it on the table. "Burn the center."

Not very specific. Iona aimed heat in a perfect circle. The paper blackened and caught flame. When the circle – perfectly round, but just slightly off from the center of the sheet – was burned out, she extinguished the fire. Once Dr. Choi leaned over to make her notes, Iona sent more heat to burn out all but a neat one inch border from the page.

"Or is this what you meant?"

"Show off. Either was acceptable." Dr. Choi took a glass from the room's mini-fridge and placed it on the table. Three ice cubes clinked against the sides of the glass. "Melt only the center cube."

"Okay. It'll melt the others if it takes too long, though." Iona focused on the one ice cube, making a thin beam of air just warm enough to heat the center of the ice. The cube folded in on itself, the liquid flowing around the bottom – still solid – ice cube.

Dr. Choi tapped her notes. "Admirable control. I think we have enough for a baseline. Up to sixteen hours and your control is nearly perfect. After that, it decreases slowly for another ten hours. After twenty-six hours, it falls apart." She checked her notes. "It's been six hours since your last orgasm. You'll be fine to make a quick field mission. Report to Morrison for details."

Already? Iona hopped off the stool. "A real mission, or another test?"

"We're short-handed. He asked for you. You ready?"

"All charged up." Iona held out her hands. As if the heat she controlled was visible. "Quick means just a few hours, right? I don't need to pack a bag?"

"You know as well as I do what can happen. Take what you think you'll need for double the time you might be out."

Iona stopped at her quarters on the medical level. Real shoes instead of med-level slippers. A jacket in case of rain. A mini vibrator in case she was out past that twenty-six hour deadline. Her phone – fully charged for a change. All set.

Her phone chimed as she waited for the elevator. She slid her thumb across the screen. A text from Morrison telling her to meet in his briefing room. First floor then.

Morrison – tall, broad, and dark – sat alone at a table with two open chairs when she entered. "Welcome back, Sinclair."

"Solo mission?"

Morrison tapped a finger on the table. "He's late. Medical says you're okay in the field as long as you take precautions." He focused his gaze on her. "You have those precautions in hand?"

She nodded. Without giggling. Doc would be proud of her.

"Good," Morrison continued. "Johansen sucks at punctuality, but I'd like him back un–burnt." He waited until she nodded again, then pointed at one of the chairs across from him. As she sat, he asked, "Are you up to date on current events?"

Sven Johansen. Only one agent by that name. Infamous for his good looks and charming personality. "I guess you don't mean basketball scores." She shrugged. "Local news, some Amp news, and news that filters in downstairs. More reports on rogues, maybe an organized group. That why we're short-handed?" Bits and pieces of various conversations popped into her mind. Amps who didn't want to be regulated, pheno Amps who didn't want to live in gated communities away from normals. All people the Bureau had to deal with.

"We're not short-handed. Just busy. Everyone's got an assignment and we need every able-bodied officer out there in the field."

A tall blond man swung the door open and joined them. Morrison was broad-shouldered... but Sven was straight from central casting for a Viking flick.

Morrison pointedly checked the time. "You're late. Sinclair, Johansen is backup and your liaison with base this mission. Johansen, she'll take point." He pointed behind Sven. "Close the door."

Sven got back up and pressed the door shut with a click. He sat in the open chair with a grin for Iona. "Rogues again?"

Morrison switched on the projector. A map blossomed on the wall. Sven scraped his chair around to face it.

"This is their target. The city's last uncovered water reservoir."

Sven raised his hand. "This is where I ask, again, why they haven't covered it yet."

"Time and money. Same as always." Morrison circled the reservoir with his laser pointer. "The rogues are getting organized. They've sent a demand that they want the Bureau to publicly announce by seventeen hundred hours or they'll freeze the city water supply. A manipulator Amp – calls himself Cube – will be there to freeze the water. We don't know whether they think they can freeze the whole thing solid or whether the plan is to

freeze the incoming and outgoing pipes and burst them."
He set down the pointer. "It won't shut down all the city's
water, but it'll make a noticeable drop in our levels. We'd
rather the good citizens not be inconvenienced. More
importantly, we don't give in to terrorist demands."

"How much backup will Cube have?" Iona asked.

"We don't know for sure. There's a really good chance
that this is a distraction for something bigger going on.
We have other teams in position for the most likely of
those. Expect at least him and one other, but there could
be more. Sinclair, your primary job is to keep the water
liquid. Only tackle the rogues if you can manage it in
addition to the water. Johansen, you're communication
and muscle this time out, but any short-circuiting of their
brains would be appreciated."

Iona appraised him. He'd been in her recruitment
class, but they'd never worked a mission together. A
mental strong enough to block or mess up someone else
wasn't that common. You'd think she'd have heard that
about him by now. The bureau rumor mill usually covered
all bases.

Morrison put both hands on the table. "Any
questions?"

"Is there an image of Cube?" Iona asked.

"Here." Morrison flipped the projector to another
picture. "And go now. A car's been assigned. It's waiting
in the garage."

Iona and Sven stood. She studied Cube's picture as long as she could. Blond hair, blue eyes, narrow face, crisp jaw, blunt nose.

She nodded to Sven and stood up. "Let's do this." He stood also – he was taller than she was, but not enough to tower over her.

He led the way out and towards the elevator. "Okay if I drive?" he asked. "I know a shortcut."

"Fine by me. Can we stop for dinner on the way back?"

He stabbed the elevator button. "There's a couple of diners along the shortcut. One Chinese place and one steakhouse."

"Either's fine." She tugged her shoulder pack back into place. "Will your shortcut get us there ahead of the bad guys?"

They entered the empty elevator. "The way I drive it will." He grinned. Maybe he was kidding? "We know their plan and that Cube hasn't left their headquarters yet. We're closer to the reservoir than they are."

The elevator door slid open onto the parking level. "Why do I get the feeling you know more about this mission than I do?"

Sven pointed to a bright blue sports car. "Sweet ride, huh?"

"Not exactly camouflage."

"Undercover as a couple out on a picnic." He opened the passenger door for her.

"A couple?" She swung her pack onto the floor before ducking into the car.

He closed her door, came around the back, and got into the driver's seat. The key, already in the ignition, dangled a shiny gold fob shaped like a smiley face. Sven started the car and sighed. "Listen to that engine."

"Morrison didn't say this was an undercover operation."

He grinned. "Doesn't mean we can't make it one. Look in the back."

Wedged behind his seat was an actual picnic basket. "You packed a lunch?"

"Not quite. I added it to the car requisition. It'll be a late lunch, but we can still stop for dinner on the way back." He drove out of the garage and signaled to turn onto the street. "I know you don't date Amps, but—"

"What? I've dated Amps."

"That's not the word around the office."

Of course he'd heard tales about her.

This shit again? "Maybe I don't date guys in the Bureau because I don't want my dating life to be office gossip," she snapped. At least these tales kept all but the most persistent from asking her out. She glanced over at her partner of the day. He was easy on the eyes and should be her type: tall, charming, quick to smile.

Sven pulled onto the freeway. "Sorry. I was just trying to make it not-weird that we go on a pretend picnic." He signaled and moved into the center lane.

"It's fine." Iona watched the traffic, hoping the conversation was over. Afternoon rush hour was getting started. "What's this shortcut of yours?"

"We'll take the next exit." Sven pointed with hands still on the wheel. "There's a road there that comes out at the back of the reservoir."

"And a picnic place?"

"Haven't you been there?" He grinned again. There was a dimple she hadn't noticed. "Outside the fence, there's a grassy lawn with benches and trees. A few beds of roses. Very romantic." He exited the freeway. Just past the typical gas station and fast food places, forest crowded close to the sides of the road. "Okay, word from HQ – Cube is on the move."

"What did Morrison mean about you scrambling their minds? I've worked with telepaths, but they couldn't do that. How powerful are you?" Shoulders and dimples notwithstanding.

"As telepaths go, I'm not all that useful. I can only 'path with Carlos. He'll be talking to the telepaths watching our target and the teams working the other events we have leads on. When he and I work together, we can confuse someone, muddy their thinking for a bit. It's not always a guaranteed effect, though. Even better – when we put our minds to it, we're telekinetic."

Carlos Martinez, she remembered better than Sven, from their bureau orientation courses. Shorter than Sven with a sweet smile. Didn't talk much. "So maybe this muddying can distract the target, or his handler, while I keep things from freezing." Almost a plan. "Or you can drop a tree on him." Iona checked the dashboard clock.

An hour since she left the infirmary. Stop the bad guy, grab a quick dinner, and then home in time for bed.

The forested hillside gave way to cleared land along the ridge. Golf course on one side, cemetery on the other. Houses just down the slope, still high enough for a view of the cityscape.

"Your power's fire, right, not just heat?"

"Yep." Iona held her hands up, fingers spread, and let a tiny flame dance atop one index finger. She extinguished the fire before Sven could complain about danger to the upholstery.

He controlled his double-take well. The car barely swerved. "Cool." He glanced over again. "That's why the field name and the red hair, then."

Iona stifled a groan. "It seemed *so cool* when I was fifteen. Now, I'm used to it. Can't even remember what shade of brown it used to be."

Sven reached over and flicked a lock from her shoulder. "It's a good color on you. I'm not one to talk. Carlos and I used to try and invent our own language until someone pointed out that telepathy meant no one else could hear us."

"You and he have always been able to talk to each other?" A sign said '*Skyline Reservoir next right*'.

He turned onto the side road. "Yeah. We were born same day, at the same time – not quite to the minute, but close – at the same bureau hospital. We were always in each other's heads. Mom and Dad thought he was my imaginary friend for the longest time." That grin again.

"Eventually, they figured out I was a mental and that I could only use my power with Carlos, and he with me."

The road curved up through neatly mowed greenspaces. A tiny gravel parking lot was empty except for a car with a bike rack parked in the shade of a tree.

"What's the latest word on where our target is and whether he has anyone with him?"

Sven backed into the space closest to the exit and turned off the engine. "Checking now."

In the silence, Iona scanned the area. Nobody was visible between the parking lot and the high wrought-iron fence around the reservoir. The larger parking area from Morrison's map was a grey shimmer at the opposite end of the water.

"We made it," Sven said. He got out of the car and stretched.

"Well?"

He reached behind his seat and pulled the picnic basket free. "There's a nice spot in the sunshine over there. Good place to set up the blanket."

Still no one around. Iona pushed the car door open just as Sven reached the door and held out his hand to help her out. "Have you worked with someone you weren't telepathically linked before? You know you have to talk to the rest of us, right?"

He smiled.

Those stupid dimples.

"I'm hungry. Let's get the picnic setup then I'll fill you in." He lifted the basket and took her hand.

She let him lead the way to a level place close to the reservoir fence but a straight shot back to the car. Inside the basket was a traditional red checkered tablecloth that he shook out dramatically and let fall more or less smoothly onto the grass.

"Fine." Iona sat on the cloth, facing the water. "What's in the basket?"

Sven opened the basket, put the insulating cover aside, and unpacked a series of covered bowls. He lifted the first lid. "Fried chicken. You're not a vegetarian, are you?"

"Not this week."

He gave her a look – sideways through his eyelashes – and passed her the bowl.

"They must have known it would be you." He set the next bowl down. "Greek salad."

"Why is that me?" Plates. They'd need plates. She took a cold drumstick anyway.

"Greek." He waved the hand holding the lid to the salad. "Your name?"

She shook her head. "Not Greek. Mum just liked the name."

"Ah-ha. You're English then." He finally pulled two plates and sets of utensils out.

Someplace to put her chicken. "Nope. American. Mum is from Canada. Any more questions?"

"Sorry, just like to get to know my partners. Something to talk about, you know. My folks were recruited from Sweden, Carlos's mom from Mexico."

She waited until he had chicken, salad, and biscuits on his plate. "Didn't we cover all that back in orientation? Okay, now can you let me know what you've heard from headquarters?"

His mouth was full. Chew, chew, and swallow. "That was what, five years ago? Anyway, Cube and a woman are in a little blue pickup. Don't know her name or her power type, but she has freakishly fast reflexes. Best guess is that it is sense, premonition, or muscle-speed." He tore off another bite of chicken. "Sorry," he said around the mouthful. "I skipped breakfast."

No pickup trucks, blue or otherwise were on the road at either end of the park.

Sven swallowed. "Traffic cameras have them on the freeway, two exits away. Eat up." He finished the piece of chicken. "So, Canadian mum. Dad around?"

"Never met him."

"Typical Amp. One of the Bureau-arranged marriages and pregnancies? Glad they've stopped doing that."

"Don't be so sure they stopped." Doc Choi would love to pair her up with Amps of specific talents, just to see what skills the offspring would have. *Wonder if she'd just let me donate a batch of eggs?* She only met other amps at work, and her dating history with normals was a series of disasters. A regular, healthy relationship would be nice for a change. "They still offer plenty of incentives if we want to have kids. Long family leave, full pay with bonuses. It's not as shadowy, but they still want us breeding the next generation of amps with fancy superpower." Iona put empty containers back in the basket. "Your turn. Parents?"

"Both Swedish, emigrated under the Bureau recruitment drive when they were just out of high school. They already knew each other and married during college. Dad's a telepath, Mom's a water manipulator." He tossed the last bowl into the basket and popped to his feet. "Time to move, they've left the freeway. Orders are not to engage until the talks with the rogues have completely broken down."

Iona let him help her up, but pulled her hand free upon standing.

"You haven't done much undercover, have you?"

"Once they need me, the situation's kind of past stealth."

He grabbed the picnic blanket by one corner and wadded it into a ball. Dropping it in the basket, he held out his hand. "Stay at my side, pretend like you like it. We'll stroll over to the roses there—" he pointed "—then wander closer to the water while they're driving in. How close do you need to get?"

Iona shrugged. "Closer is better for accuracy. It depends on how he works. If he needs to touch or point at the water, I have to have a sightline between him and the water. If he just needs to think about it, I can be anywhere in the vicinity." She put an arm around his waist and snuggled up to his side. "I might not do much undercover, but I know how to date."

Sven chuckled and wrapped an arm around her shoulders. "That you do."

They walked over to the closest rose garden. Flower, flower, flower, spider. No blue pickup yet. Another flower. "Did your folks know Carlos's mom before you were born, or not until you discovered you were linked?"

"His mom was part of the same recruiting class as my parents. She's a weather pre-cog and worked with my mom a lot. She'd predict the storms and Mom would redirect the water for less damage."

"Neat partnership." Sven was the perfect height for snuggling while walking. His arm was warm across her shoulders. He even smelled good. Even with her rule about dating co-workers, it didn't mean she'd never been attracted. He should be perfect. So why didn't she feel anything but his warmth?

"Here's one for you," Sven said, stopping at a bush with brilliant orange-red roses. He tapped a foot at the marker in the ground. *'Flame On'*. "It's named for you. You should get one for your garden."

Shit. He's thoughtful too. Was being sexually self-sufficient making her unresponsive to real live men? That would suck. She leaned her head against his shoulder. "My apartment balcony was a bit small for a rose garden."

"There's the truck."

Yep. Little and blue. They strolled along the roses, heads bowed together but glancing past the water as the truck parked and its doors opened. "Towards the fence now?"

"Sure." She kept her head against his shoulder. The muscles under his skin were every bit as firm as they looked. Across the reservoir, the amp who must be Cube was approaching the fence. Good guys on one end, bad guys on the other. Great setting for a stand-off. Just a fenced pool of water between them.

A clatter from the parking lot near their car pulled her attention from the bad guys. *There aren't more of them, are there?* A quick look was enough to see a bicyclist loading his mountain bike back on his car.

"Think they'll hold off until he's gone?" she murmured into his chest.

"If they did, they'd wait for us to leave, too. And we aren't going anywhere. The surveillance team didn't say how short his fuse is. Or hers."

Cube's partner, bodyguard, whatever, joined him. From this distance, Iona didn't see more than light hair and a blue jacket.

Sven steered her towards the corner of the fence. They slowed and meandered, keeping their faces tilted towards one another. From a distance, she hoped they'd look absorbed and in love.

"Are they going to cut the fence?" Sven asked.

Iona led him back from the corner and leaned her shoulder against the fence where she had a view of the length of the water. "I don't think so. They stopped a few feet away. Unless her power includes cutting metal, they don't have the tools with them."

Sven stood at her other shoulder, close enough to snuggle against. "How cold would he have to get it for the fence to get brittle enough to break?"

"Way colder than humans can tolerate."

"So you don't know."

She shrugged against his chest. He was warm, strong, and just the right size. But no sparks or chemistry at all. "Not precisely."

"They said until 17:00. How close are we?"

She checked her phone. "Almost an hour to go. Can you sense any telepathic powers from them, or are they waiting for a phone call?"

"No way to tell if anyone's talking to them. Not on my frequency." He leaned close and nuzzled her neck. "They're looking this way."

Iona tilted her face up to meet his lips. "Remember, I'm playing undercover agent," she said before she kissed him.

He knew what he was doing. Why wouldn't her body respond?

He pulled back just far enough to whisper, "Noted." Another brief kiss. "But, I must say, you're very good at this."

"Thank you. I think they're not watching now."

She pulled her face away from his, but nestled against his side. Maybe Doc Choi could send her for counseling to fix whatever was wrong with her head. Maybe what happened with Brad broke her. She hadn't even pretended to rub Sven's back. It felt like she still had control of the fire. She glanced over Sven's shoulder. The bicyclist's car was gone.

"Keep an eye on them," she said and turned her back on Cube and his partner. She wrapped one arm around Sven's stomach and held her free hand where her body shielded it from the bad guys. With a touch of concentration, a small flame bloomed on her palm. She danced it up and down each finger, grew it larger, and shrank it back down.

"Whatcha doing?" Sven asked.

"Just testing." She made a fist and closed up the fire. "My control should be fine until midnight, at least. Just making sure."

"Ah. Word from headquarters. The rogues have repeated their threats. We're not the only game in town. They're talking about a tornado south of town, disruption on the bridges, and phenos in crowded parks."

She turned back around. Still just them and the pair of bad guys on the reservoir grounds. Freezing the water supply wasn't going to be immediately obvious to the public. She wasn't going to let it happen anyway. "We should look at the roses some more. Can you ask headquarters to make sure all the pipes in and out of the reservoir are metal, not plastic? I want an idea of how hot I can make things."

They walked between the rows of rose bushes. Iona paused and sniffed each variety and pointed at random blooms without comment.

"Got your answer," Sven said. "It's old enough that all the pipes are copper. As long as you know the melting point and don't go above it, you'll be fine."

"I can always send Cube a message and cover the water with a blanket of fire."

"They'll certainly know we're here."

A gust of wind blew through, whipping Iona's hair across her face and sending leaves dancing in a swirl.

She raked her hair back. "A little more of that wind might keep them distracted."

He glanced through the fence at their opponents. "I don't think it bothered them. But, if it were fall, Carlos and I could make a mess and keep them from seeing us."

"Sorry. It was an idea."

"A decent one. Once they make a move, and I can see what they're doing, maybe there's something we can do to block them while you keep the water warm." He wrapped his arm around her shoulder and she leaned against his solid warmth. There was definitely something wrong with her if he wasn't turning her on. He checked all her boxes – charming, tall, good-looking, sense of humor, smart enough but not arrogant about it – there just wasn't any chemistry.

A chill rose up from the water, cooling the surrounding air. Cube held his hands out, facing the water.

Iona shook her hands out. "They're starting early. Which do we want, a gentle warming or a blanket of flame?"

Sven grinned at her. "Let's show them who they're up against."

Iona held her hands out like she was admiring her nail polish or showing off a ring. Warmth formed in the center of her palms and she visualized it flowing out towards the still-cooling water. She returned the smile. "I'll warm it a bit, then show them some flames."

At the far end of the reservoir, nearest Cube, the glitter of ice formed on the water's surface. The heat Iona sent had just reached the edge of the ice when Sven grabbed her hands.

"Stop."

NoNoNoNoNo. Extinguish hands. Don't burn him. She snatched her hands away, hugging them around her body. "Never grab my hands. Are you an idiot?"

One of them had yelled loudly enough to attract Cube's attention.

Iona leaned on Sven. "Crap. They're looking. Pretend to comfort me or something. Just don't touch my hands."

"I promise." He wrapped an arm around her shoulders. "Sorry. They're filming."

"They're what?"

"Filming. The other one has a camera. Or a phone. She was aiming it at his hands and the water. They figured out you were warming the water and pointed the camera at us."

"No flames then." She turned one hand palm outward, keeping her arms across her body. "I'll push some heat across to the end he's freezing. Can you and Carlos use some telekinesis to mess up their filming? Make her drop the camera or blow some leaves in her way or something?"

"Good idea." He kept his arm around her.

Her hand was the focus, her mind pushed heat into and across the water. The glitter of ice faded into ripples as she defeated the chill. The camera was obvious now, held aloft in the woman's hands. A paper blew across the grass and flipped up to flatten against the front of the camera. Nothing else moved in the still air.

"Good job," she said to Sven.

"Eh, wasn't very natural looking." A trail of leaves from beneath the shrubs lining the fence twirled up past the pair trying to freeze the water.

Iona's hand wavered. With her arm against her body, Cube wouldn't be able to tell, but she was weakening. "Do they look bored yet?"

"Not bored," Sven said.

The camera crashed to the ground.

"You and Carlos?"

Sven grunted an affirmative sound.

"Nice work." Iona lowered the temp she sent to the water, keeping it around air temperature.

Cube thrust his arms down at his sides.

"Now they looked pissed."

"As long as he stops trying to make ice." Iona eased back on the heat. This steady control was harder than a blast of flame. But she was keeping control.

"Uh oh."

"What?" she tossed her hair back to see.

"They're coming. Will the water stay warm enough if we wander back to the car?"

Iona flicked her fingers wide and shook out her hand, sending the fire within to dormancy. "Until he tries again."

"You!" Cube shouted and broke into a run. He shot his arm forward and an icy blast shot past Iona, blowing her hair back from her face.

Sven pressed his hand on Iona's back. "Run. He's pushing the car."

Still alone in the little parking lot, the car moved along the pavement towards the strip of grass separating the lot from the road. If Cube or his partner were making the car move, it wasn't likely grass would stop it.

CHAPTER TWO

Iona kept up with Sven as they raced for the car. The sheen of ice glittered on the pavement and their little sports car was gaining speed across the lot. She glanced back. Cube was still coming, his partner zipping ahead, behind, and from one side to the other. Covering him, probably.

She could warm the pavement as easily as the water. Palms out, she pushed heat at the ground surrounding the car as she ran. Not enough to hurt the car or explode the gas tank, just enough to get things above freezing. A few yards closer and she focused on the area in front of the car.

One tire caught de-iced pavement and the rear end skewed sideways. More heat in front of each tire. Shit. One palm flamed just for a moment, the heat beam caught a rear tire and it popped and flattened.

"Sorry."

Sven was still at her side. He looked back, then at the car. "Good job. You kept it from crashing. Two cars are coming up the road now."

She'd been so focused on melting the ice, she hadn't noticed the cars coming. One engine-revving sports car and one diesel-sounding engine. Rubbing her hands together to dissipate the heat, she slowed to a stop. "What do we do about Cube with witnesses around?"

Sven kept walking to the car. "He already decided to split."

Iona whirled around. Cube and his partner were nearly to their truck. "Headquarters want us to stop them?"

The arriving cars parked closer to the roses and two couples emerged. Sven squatted beside the flat tire and she joined him. He shook his head. *At her question, or at the tire?* "They'd rather follow Cube back. The better to watch for their next move. Have you ever changed a tire?"

Spots of heat hadn't left her palms. She held them out and flames erupted. "Yes, but it's not a good idea right now." Something glinted behind the tire. Not ice, metal. "That's what did it. That bottle cap. My heat flared and must have superheated the metal enough to pop the tire."

"You okay now?"

"Yeah. I mean I am, but my control is shot. I shouldn't be this bad already. My control should have lasted until midnight. I don't trust the fire now. We need to recalibrate."

"Noted – no more fire today. Good thing ice hands took off." He flashed another of those be-dimpled grins at her and opened the trunk. "Jackpot. There's a real tire in here. Is that 'we' you and me or someone back at the infirmary?"

"Infirmary. We'd figured I had sixteen hours before losing control." She fisted her hands to keep the heat inside. "But using it to keep a steady warmth instead of blast of flame takes more control. We didn't figure that would use up my safety margin."

"We'll get you back there once this is fixed. You'd better stay away from flammable things until then."

Sitting on the grass was out of the question. Iona knelt, then twisted her legs until she was sitting cross-legged on the pavement, without using her hands for balance. The fire felt like it filled her palms, right under the skin. She took several deep breaths to calm it. Sometimes that helped.

Not this time. The weird unsettled feeling connected her center to her hands. All these weeks of practice made it easy to recognize. Giggles came across the lawn from the couples at the rose bushes. It looked like a photo shoot. The couples took turns posing by the roses and by the cars – an older diesel Mercedes and a newer Corvette.

Metal clanged to the pavement by her knee, making her jump. Sven had his hands full of the jack and had dropped the four-way tire iron.

"Hand me that, would you?" Sven held out a hand. "No, not hand. Can you kick it over?"

"Better idea." A careful nudge with one foot sent the iron sliding over to the flat tire and Sven got to work loosening the lug nuts.

Those couples looked happy, and normal. One couple, a man and woman with dark skin were leaning against the

Mercedes while the other couple – a white woman with dark blond hair and one with medium-toned skin and glossy straight black hair, directed and took their picture. Then the first woman took pictures of the other two women lounging together on the hood of the Corvette. "Wouldn't it be nice to be able to have a normal job and a normal relationship?"

"Huh?" Sven grunted as he spoke, pumping the handle of the jack to lift the car.

She nodded in the direction of the photo shoot. "Like them. No worries about uncontrolled powers, or rogues trying to upset the Bureau."

He glanced over. "How do you know they're normals? Not all of us work for the Bureau. And normals have just as many relationship problems."

"I guess." Iona leaned back, putting her hands on the pavement for support. Heat rushed out and she snatched them back. "Dammit. I need to get this under control."

Sven wrestled the tire off. "Will you make it back to the infirmary without losing control? The car's checked out in my name."

He made it sound like a joke, but it wasn't something she took lightly.

"Maybe not. If there were someplace here I could have some privacy, I brought supplies to help." Two glassy spots on the pavement proved her fire wasn't under control. One was palm-sized, but the one from her right hand included enough of her fingers to be an obvious handprint. Deliberately, she hovered her hand over the spot and shot enough heat out to blur the spot into a glassy blob.

Hands carefully together, she watched the couples taking pictures. Even if they were amps, it looked like a pleasantly normal way to spend an afternoon. Even though she wasn't helping, changing a flat tire was something normal people did. It was part of a normal life.

Sven rolled the spare tire into position and heaved it up onto the bolts. He felt around for the tire iron, then turned to look for it and met her eyes. "What?"

"Just thinking that maybe this makes us a little more normal after all."

"Told you. Normal is what you make of it."

Iona examined her hands "Yeah, but some of us are less normal that others."

He finger-tightened the lug nuts, then lowered the car until the tire rested on the ground before finishing with the wrench. "How private? The car's doors lock, but the windows aren't tinted."

"Better in the car than behind a bush." She sighed and looked across at the treetops. "I need regular orgasms to keep the fire under control."

He kept his eyes on the tire, bright spots of color blooming on his cheeks. "There is nothing I can say after that that won't be creepy." He tested each lug nut again. "We can throw the picnic blanket over the car to block the windows. I'll go see if Cube left any clues behind."

"Thank you."

Sven returned the lug wrench and jack to the car's tiny trunk and piled the flat tire on top of them. "Sit tight while I get the basket." He strode across to where the basket and blanket sat undisturbed on the grass.

Such a nice view he presented, why wasn't her body interested? Or her brain. Which was the bigger problem here? The couples were huddled together and giggling. Two of them looked over at Sven, but turned back to their camera and continued giggling. By the time he returned, and the view was just as good from the front, the couples were heading back to their cars.

Sven tossed the picnic basket into the space behind the driver's seat and flicked out the blanket so it covered the car's roof and windows. He opened the door and arranged the blanket so it hung inside and closed the door on it.

"Okay, ready for you now." He crossed the front of the car and opened the passenger door. "Go ahead and get in. The keys are on the driver's seat. I'll lock the door after I tuck the blanket in on this side. And I'll put the wipers on top of it too, just in case of wind."

She pressed her knuckles onto the pavement and rocked up onto her feet. "Thank you."

"Let me know when you're ready to leave. I'll be over there somewhere." He waved a hand in the direction of the reservoir.

The other cars started with only a little extra revving of their engines and they headed past them and onto the road.

"Good timing." Iona steadied her breath. The fire felt calmer. Just a bit.

Sven closed her door gently.

Iona willed the fire to stay down and got the mini vibrator from her bag. Her jeans weren't tight, but pulling them off in this cramped car didn't seem like it would add to the experience. She refused to think about any men she knew, but imagined warm hands caressing her body. Hands that knew what she liked best, soft touches feather-light over her most sensitive areas, rubbing the lace of her bra against her skin, teasing the edges of her panties.

She powered on the vibrator and eased it along the path of those imagined hands. Small circles on either side of the zipper on her pants. She switched hands and touched the lever to recline the seat. With legs apart, she rolled the vibrator back and forth along either side of her crotch. The seam below the zipper right where she needed the action. She tested the vibration against the seam itself and rocked it against her clitoris.

Those imaginary hands were joined by an imaginary tongue and lips. Whoever she was imagining was very good with them and her breath came faster. She closed her eyes and let her lips part as she moved the vibrator faster, up and down against her jeans. Holding back wasn't the point. She rocked her hips in time with her panting, clenching the interior muscles rhythmically.

Faster again, the vibrator, the panting, and her hips until the release came in waves. She let her hand drop away. The imaginary hands stroked her cheek and caressed her shoulder before vanishing. He was good, this imaginary lover of hers. Not good enough to permanently replace a flesh-and-blood lover, but awfully good in the meantime.

She raised the seat back and checked on the fire. That was the real test. It lay dormant like it was supposed to. She unlocked the door and slid out. Their little car was still alone in the parking lot. A few safe steps away and she called up the fire to dance on her finger tip. Just a tiny candle-sized flame, just enough to prove control. She smiled at it and sent it away.

Sven was on the far side of the reservoir, looking intently at the ground. Iona untucked the blanket from both doors and wipers, folded it, and put it with the basket. During all that, Sven headed back to the car.

When he was close enough to hear, she asked, "Find anything?"

"Not really. A cupcake wrapper that may or may not have fallen from their truck. Tire tracks. Some leaves with blackened edges from the cold. Everything okay here?"

"All ready to go. Fire's under control."

He glanced at the sky. "I think we talked about dinner earlier? We should be able to beat the dinner rush if we go now."

He climbed in first and his cheeks reddened as bright as her hair.

The little silver vibrator was still on her seat. She covered it with her hand as she sat and swept it into her bag.

"High school must have sucked," Sven said as he started the car. "Dealing with that."

She figured out which 'that' he meant. "Oh. It wasn't a problem back then. The fire was well-behaved until I joined the Bureau and started using it all the time. It's not a practical side effect – the more I use it, the less control I have. And 'that' isn't the only way to fix the lack of control. The doc wired me up and found several points in my brain to stimulate that also worked. Away from the infirmary though, this is easier. Something I can do myself."

All by myself. All alone. Hooray for self-sufficiency.

Alone sucked.

"Uh oh," Sven said. "Can we postpone the dinner? Carlos said we're being called in for a team briefing."

They hadn't even reached the main road.

CHAPTER THREE

"Sorry about the dinner," Sven said for the third time as they headed to the stairwell leading up from the underground parking garage.

Iona just nodded. Again. "It's okay. All part of the job. Hopefully we'll just get our assignments for tomorrow and we're done for the day." They passed both basement levels and the first floor landing and he kept going. "Where's the meeting?"

"Second floor conference room." He paused for her at the half-way landing. "Carlos just said they're waiting for us so they can start."

Iona raked her hair back from her face and pulled open the second floor door for Sven. He swept past with a thanks and reached the conference room first to hold the door for her. "After you this time."

The room wasn't quite full, but close. Iona took the empty seat beside Lisa Wong-Osunbar and Sven sat across from her between the telepath Broadcast and Sven's partner-in-telepathy, Carlos.

Broadcast – the only agent she knew who only went by his field name, never by his real name – raised his eyebrows at Sven. "About time you showed up."

Any response Sven made was telepathic.

As the door latched with a click that echoed through the now-silent room, two men stood at the head of the table; Morrison, and a pheno amp with red crystalline skin.

"Okay," Morrison said, leaning both hands on the back of his chair. "Now that Flame and Left are here, let's get started."

Task Force meeting meant Morrison was using field names. She hadn't noticed if he was left-handed. His field name must mean something else. It might mean something paired with Carlos's field name

Morrison continued, "All of you were out today to contain the same coordinated actions. The group calling itself the Freedom Movement orchestrated several high-visibility events that they wanted to film and broadcast live. Flame and Left managed to interrupt the rogues trying to freeze an open reservoir and film it. Lassie and another team were south of town where several pheno rogues acted the part of Bigfoot for their cameras. The team was able to track the rogues and contain them. Their cameras were confiscated and our technicians here scrambled the feed before it could be uploaded."

A laugh-snort sounded in Iona's head. One of the telepaths. The sound matched the smirk on Broadcast's face. Morrison stared him down until Broadcast spoke aloud.

"If by 'technicians' you mean two telepaths, a super-magnet-man, and Tami who can talk to computers."

"Yes," Morrison said. "Our technical team was able to prevent the broadcast."

Hard to be sure with Morrison, but maybe he used Cast's field name intentionally there.

Cast grinned. "Do I get a raise for doing technical work?"

"No. Anyone else have a smart ass remark?"

A few people shifted in their seats and Sven muffled a cough that sounded suspiciously like 'Cast's an ass'.

Morrison stretched to his full height, well over six feet tall, and aimed a remote at the screen on the wall. With a laser pointer, he indicated an area west of town. "Here, the Freedom Movement created two small tornados. They were able to present a live broadcast online of the tornados, but without proof they were anything other than natural phenomena. We had Breeze and Lift on scene to minimize injuries or property damage. Local meteorologists are reporting them as the result of sudden air pressure changes." He moved the laser pointer to circle the downtown area and all the bridges there. "Traffic was impacted here when they managed to lower the lift gates on most of the bridges. Two of the bridges started to raise, but were stopped in time. City officials are reporting it as a computer or electrical malfunction, but aren't squashing rumors of terrorism or malicious mischief."

Iona raised her hand and waited for Morrison to nod in her direction. "At the reservoir, Left noticed that the Movement rogues weren't trying to film their actions, but ours."

Sven nodded. "That's right, the way she held the camera, it wouldn't have shown more than Cube's hands and the water. When they spotted us, she aimed the camera at Flame."

"Interesting," Morrison pressed his lips together. "So they want the public to know about amps with powers, but ours, not theirs. So all the public outcry will come our way." He turned to the red-crystal man. "Manik is co-head of this task force, dealing specifically with any rogue phenos we encounter. Do we have statements from any of them that might be useful?"

Manik tilted his head to one side. "Nothing more than their propaganda pamphlets and websites include. Once the three who were playing Bigfoot are brought in, maybe we'll have more." He gestured to the green-skinned woman seated closest to him. "Gator is my number two for the task force. If you contain any phenos belonging to the Freedom Movement, bring them to both of our attentions. She'll assign resources to interrogate or assimilate them."

Sven raised his hand. "What's the rule on contain or let escape? We were told to let Cube go."

Manik gestured for Morrison to answer.

"It's case by case. Our surveillance team—Bark, Lucent, and Shadow— are watching what we think is the main headquarters of the group. Letting the members we know about come and go lets us gather more information about their plans. Lucent? Is someone watching now?"

A voice from along the wall under the window answered. "Shadow is there now. Once it's fully dark, Bark will take over. I have the daylight hours."

Morrison nodded. "Good. I expect there to be more activity after today's attempts."

Iona couldn't see Lucent along the wall. Another man was entirely the color of the light wood trim surrounding the window. Camouflage amps.

Tami-who-talks-to-computers raised her hand. "Their forums and video channels all blew up today. Do you want us to keep suppressing the same ones and letting the others through?"

Morrison nodded. "Good question, Byte. It's been working to throttle or erase the more reasonable-looking of their sites and let the paranoid-looking ones through. If we stop all of them, they'll be more suspicious. Keep us apprised of any changes in their sites and monitor the comment sections." He glared at Cast. "All of the technical team can monitor. Get anyone else not busy to help, too."

Cast shrugged. "Sure. What about the TV show? Can we help with that too?"

Iona straightened in her seat. She'd been out of the loop for a while.

Morrison sighed. "The staff is already assigned. You aren't needed." He looked around the table. "For those who haven't heard yet, the bureau is participating in the production of a new television show about film-making tricks. We have amps in most of the writing and production positions, and normals in the on-camera roles. They'll be showing how special effects are done, and we'll make sure most of them show things that the Freedom Movement can claim to be done by amps."

From the murmurs around the table, Iona wasn't the only one who hadn't heard of the show yet.

"Any other questions?" Morrison asked. "The surveillance and technical teams have their assignments. Left and Right are telepaths on call in case anyone needs them. The rest of you will get some based on what they discover. Thanks for your hard work today."

That answered the question of how their field names were related. Not super imaginative, but most weren't. As some people stood and others chatted, Lisa nudged Iona and leaned close. "So, a field assignment. Does this mean the doc released you?"

"Not yet. After I give today's report, we might have to make some adjustments."

"Want to meet for dinner later? I'll pick something up if you're staying in." At Iona's nod, Lisa pushed her seat back. "Let me just check with someone." Lisa went over to the windows where the surveillance team stood.

Sven cleared his throat and Iona looked across the table at him.

"I want to introduce you to the other half of my brain. Again, I guess. Iona, Carlos, Carlos, Iona." He gestured from her to the man at his side and back.

Carlos, handsome in a shy, sweet kind of way, stuck out his hand. "Nice to see you again." He had wavy black hair and the tiniest hint of dimples when he spoke.

Almost too late, she reached across the table to shake the offered hand. "Likewise. Thanks for the support today."

"You're welcome. I never get away from this guy, so it's nice when he has someone else along."

Lisa dropped back into her seat. "Hey Carlos." She didn't mention Sven and focused on Iona. "Okay, dinner then? Chinese or Thai?"

"Close Chinese or good Chinese?"

"The place across the street."

"Thai. Give me time in case the doc needs to meet after she sees my report."

"Sure. I need to finish my report before I get the food. See you then." Lisa headed out of the room. Footsteps and the breeze from passing bodies followed Lisa out. *The camo phenos have left the room.*

Sven plopped both palms on the table. Reports for me too. Want me to copy you on mine?"

"Sure." She tried to keep the relief out of her voice. He'd be within his rights to include her near loss of control. At least he wasn't going to try to hide what he wrote. They all rose from the table and left the room together.

As they passed the head of the table, Morrison spoke, "Good job today, Flame. Hope they'll release you to us full time soon."

"Me, too," seemed like the best answer. Better than *'I hope I can handle it'*, anyway.

Sven and Carlos trailed her as far as the elevators where she jabbed the down button. "We're on this floor," Sven said. "Glad I got to work with you today. If we're all stuck working in the office on the same day, we should try to get lunch together."

"I'd like that."

Carlos held out a hand. "I hope I get to work with you soon."

She shook his hand. His grip was steady and gentle. "We're on the same task force, so it's likely."

"Most of the bureau is on this team," Carlos answered.

"Good point." The elevator dinged its arrival and doors slid open. "My ride is here. Goodnight."

The sub-basement was divided between infirmary, research, and a few containment cells. Iona's infirmary suite was designed for amps who needed medical monitoring, but were otherwise healthy. She had separate working and sleeping areas, her own bathroom, and a mini-kitchenette. Still, she missed having her own apartment.

The artificial sunlight was still at daytime levels, but activity on the floor was quieter than day shift. "Welcome back," Nancy at the information desk said. "Doctor Choi wants you to check in right away."

Iona thanked her without rolling her eyes and turned left to the offices instead of right to her rooms. Doc Choi's door was ajar so Iona rapped once and pushed it open. "You wanted to see me before I wrote my reports?"

"Sit down." Doctor Amanda Choi was short and stout with piercing eyes and hair that was in a slightly different bun every day. She jabbed a pen in Iona's direction. "I'd like to leave in time for a dinner date so you can give me a verbal report."

The seat across the desk was hard and utilitarian, designed to prevent loitering. Iona sat with her back straight, keeping her spine away from the wooden ridges that hit her in exactly the wrong places.

"We miscalculated the difference between my creating fire and just heat. The control I needed to keep the heat at a steady level used up the time."

"Details, please. You noted the time, I expect?"

Not to the precision the doctor would prefer, but she had. Iona recounted the events of the afternoon, including the loss of control and the recovery of it.

Doc Choi nodded and took notes in pencil on a yellow legal pad, using her own form of shorthand. Despite the neat handwriting, Iona couldn't ever figure out how to read it. When Iona reached the end of the report, Choi asked questions. When did she first feel her control slipping? Could she have regained control earlier? Who made the decision to warm the water rather than blast it?

At the end, she seemed satisfied with Iona's answers. "Good job correcting the loss of control. I'll approve you for more short missions. They had you working with Sven Johansen? You worked well together?"

Iona nodded. "He's a good agent. I haven't worked with him before."

Choi made another note on her pad. "Consistency might be important. I'll suggest you work with him when possible." She looked past Iona to the wall clock. "If you add any details to your written report, flag them for me. I'll send you any notes I have in the morning."

Iona thanked her and stood to leave. A knock on the door sounded before she reached it.

Choi just said, "Go on, open it."

A lovely dark-skinned buxom woman smiled at Iona and looked past her to greet Choi. She wore a low-cut dress that showed off a magnificent dragon necklace that stretched across her chest. Iona glanced down at her own chest. Not nearly enough real estate there for something like that.

"I hope I'm not interrupting."

Choi came around her desk. "We're done here."

The women greeted each other with cheek kisses, then held hands as they followed Iona out of the office. Iona stood aside for them to pass her before she turned towards the wing with her suite. Seeing them walk jostled Iona's memory. She'd seen the woman before – Karen something or other, from the Bureau's public relations department. "Enjoy your dinner," she called out to their backs.

Her shoes were silent on the linoleum. The infirmary was quiet tonight, just air handlers and someone squeaking a swivel chair at the info desk she didn't need to pass on her way to her suite. She kicked off her shoes and left them by the door. Her laptop was charged and she took it to the couch.

She opened the file for Morrison's report first and entered the details from their encounter with Cube. Her in-box chimed just before she finished. Sven really had sent his report. She resisted the temptation to open it before sending hers.

Okay, one more sentence about how she suspected Cube used his power, then a quick edit of the whole thing. *Stupid*, she didn't need that much detail about his little truck, they already knew how to track it. Spellcheck and send.

With trepidation, she opened the report Sven sent and skimmed it. *Whew*. Nothing about her losing control of her fire. Or about how she regained that control. He'd kept his word and that wasn't trivial. Why wasn't she attracted to him? Could she have turned into the kind of person that developed physical attraction over time? No more immediately lusting after men whose looks hit all her sweet spots?

More things to talk to Choi about during her next counseling session. Things that would be out of place in her mission reports. Iona copied the report she sent Morrison and pasted it into one for the Doc, adding all the details about her fire and her use of it. Lots of details about how she could tell her control was slipping, how she dealt with that, and the consequences. Probably no one would ever notice the two shiny, extra smooth spots of asphalt in that parking lot.

"Knock, knock," Lisa said from the doorway.

"You think I'd know by now to lock my door." Iona looked up from her laptop. Spicy peanut sauce. "That smells good. Get in here."

Lisa stepped in and pushed the door closed with her hip. "It smells strong."

"Sorry. No windows to open down here."

Lisa shrugged and pulled off her jacket. "Eh, indoors always concentrates smells. I'll cope." Lisa's super-powered sense of smell made her a valuable agent for tracking the lost and missing, but came with some annoyances.

"Yeah, but I know better than to make it worse." Iona added another line to her report and sent it off to Choi's inbox. She closed her laptop and tucked it on the built-in bookcase beside the chair. "Put the food on the table and your jacket wherever." The minimally-stocked kitchen provided plates and forks, the fridge yielded a choice of beer, water, and lemonade. "Beer okay?"

"Sure. Tell me how it went out there. They sent you out with Sven? The doc's really pushing for you to get into a relationship, huh?"

"She might be, but she hasn't said anything about it since I told her it'd be a while before I was ready." Iona spooned half the food onto her plate and passed the carton to Lisa. "But you were out after faux sasquatches with the camo guys, right? How'd that go? You were the only one who could keep up with them?"

Lisa dumped the rest of the pad thai onto her plate and took a swig of beer. "Lucent and Bark? They were on stake-out at the Movement's place. I was with Cast and a sight tracker called Eagle."

"Has the team been mixed with phenos for a while?"

"Yeah." Lisa swallowed a bite. "They merged two teams a few weeks ago when we were after the same guys from two different angles."

"And it's working?"

"Some of them have limits on what they can do – like Manik and Gator. Some of them are really handy."

"You're blushing. What haven't you told me? Is your mysterious new boyfriend on the team?"

Lisa twisted her beer bottle in her hands. "We haven't told anybody yet. I wanted to wait until he met my family."

"So, it's the real thing?"

Lisa rubbed at the corner of the label until it curled away from the glass. "It's complicated."

"What relationship isn't?"

Lisa placed the bottle carefully on the table. "Promise you won't tell my parents?"

"Sure."

"I'm serious."

"I promise not to tell anyone."

Lisa leaned her elbows on the table. "It's Lucent."

"The camo pheno from the meeting?"

Lisa nodded. "Not camo though. Invisible."

"Invisible? Like, all the time."

"All the time."

"Shit. Not telling your parents makes more sense then." She ate the last two bites of dinner. "That's it. We're almost like sisters. I can be your practice introducing to family person."

"That ... might actually work. If they ask, it's the truth that you're working with both of us and met him that way. I'll talk to him and let you know." Lisa pushed her empty plate to the side. "Now, we're supposed to be talking about you on a mission with the most beautiful visible man on the team. I want details."

"You've met him, then."

"Seen him around and know his partner. Don't let them trip you up with their field names. They each use 'Left' or 'Right' at random each mission."

"Huh. Easily amused?" Sigh. "He's even better looking up close. Very nice, considerate, funny, taller than me. Should be perfect. We pretended to be a couple on a picnic date."

"I sense a 'but' coming." Lisa took another swig of beer.

"There was no attraction. No chemistry. It should have been off the charts, but I didn't feel anything." Her voice dropped to a whisper. "Do you think I'm broken? After Brad? After this?" She waved a hand to indicate the room, the infirmary, her whole control situation.

"No. You're not broken. You're allowed to take some recovery time. And maybe he's really not your type after all. Maybe he comes across as too much of a big brother for you to want to boink."

Iona very deliberately raised her eyebrows. "You've seen him, right? Most women would have to be dead to pass him up."

Lisa shrugged. "The package deal might be off-putting."

"Pretend I don't know what you're talking about. Because I don't."

"Him and Carlos. They share thoughts, feelings, and emotions. I don't know if they even can hide things from each other. Just saying."

"I didn't know it went that deep. Complications. You know Carlos? Would you trust him with secrets?"

"He's a really private person. A little shy. But, yeah, I'd trust him." Lisa peeled more of the bottle's label down. "Why? Did something happen today that you don't want him to share?"

"Today? Nah. But it's good to know in case I have other missions with either of them." Lisa might even believe that. "Now, back to you and your invisible but implied-to-be-super-hot boyfriend. When can I meet him?"

Lisa laughed. "You call that a segue? I'll talk to him and see what he thinks."

"Great. Then we can cross our fingers that the government gets around to full disclosure in our lifetime so going out in public will be possible for the two of you." Iona raised her bottle for a toast. It took Lisa a moment, but she clinked her bottle against Iona's.

"From your lips to the Government's ears." Lisa took a gulp and almost choked on it. "Notice how I said that as if we know they're not watching us already."

Iona waited until Lisa took a successful sip from her bottle. "They've been promising full disclosure at least since our parents were younger. Whatever plan they have doesn't seem to have a timeline."

"If they don't hurry up, someone like this Movement is going to force the issue. As much as I want full disclosure, doing it wrong puts targets on all our backs."

CHAPTER FOUR

Carlos balanced the pizza box and two-liter bottle of soda in one arm while fumbling for his keys as he walked up the two steps to his building. The box wobbled, tilted, and almost fell. It took both hands, but the pizza was saved. His keys, on the other hand, were in the shrubbery lining the steps.

Of the four units in the building, only one had light streaming from the windows. Luckily, it was Sven's apartment.

"Could I get a little help down here? I brought pizza."

"What kind?" Even in telepathy, Sven could sound deeply suspicious.

"Do you even have to ask?"

"I'm coming. You do know that mushrooms and Canadian bacon isn't a thing, right?"

"It's been mentioned."

Through the magic – or whatever it was – of their connection, Sven's hunger made Carlos's stomach rumble. Before he had a chance to ask what was taking so long, Sven came jogging down the steps to the entryway.

The deadbolt clicked open and Sven pulled the door inward.

"Here." Carlos thrust the pizza box at Sven. "Dropped my keys."

"It's too dark to rummage around. Use our brain."

"For keys?"

"Why not? It's not like they're heavy."

It's not like they'd ever used up their kinetic power. Exhausted themselves, but never ran out of it. Carlos pictured his keys – the black circular fob with a silver eagle embossed on it, the brass house key, the silver car key – and felt Sven's mind link with his. A faint clink in the bushes meant they'd moved them just a bit. A little more power, the sense of lightening and lifting and the keys jingled as they rolled out onto the concrete steps at Carlos's feet.

He glanced around but no one was walking past in the early evening darkness. A man retrieving the keys that fell onto the steps wouldn't look odd, anyway.

"Thanks." He lifted the soda bottle in a toast. "Want to eat at my place or yours?"

Sven opened the door to the foyer. "I've already got the game on. What took you so long?"

"Gym before pizza. It was a zoo down there. Had to wait for all the equipment. Pizza place was in and out."

Carlos slid the keys into his pocket and followed Sven up the stairs. Sven's apartment was the mirror image of his own – Sven's to the right of the staircase, his to the left. The décor wasn't the same at all. Sven leaned to modern styles with lots of chrome and black with an out-of-place blue fuzzy throw blanket usually wadded up on the couch.

Carlos preferred warm wood-tones and soft upholstery. Sven's bare wooden floors looked nice, but the deep pile of Carlos's living room rug was amazing to bare feet. They kicked off their shoes inside Sven's door and slid-skated in their socks to the couch. Carlos put the soda beside the pizza box Sven left on the coffee table.

While Sven made getting-stuff noise in the kitchen, Carlos studied the television. "Why are we watching this game? We don't like either team."

"It's the only game on tonight and our team plays both of them next month."

Good enough. Carlos sat on the edge of the couch and opened the pizza.

A three-tone deedle chirped from Carlos's pocket when he was making headway on his first slice. He wiped his hands on a paper towel and fished his phone out. Planning on a quiet night in was never a good idea when they were on call. Especially after a day with all the Freedom Movement activity. He closed the message and reported to Sven, "We're out of time for dinner. They need us back at work."

"They can't even let us finish one slice?"

"You drive, I'll carry the box."

They rushed back to Sven's car and were on the way in minutes.

"Any guesses?" Sven asked around a mouthful of pizza.

"Has to be more fallout from today."

Sven grunted what sounded like agreement.

The underground parking at the office was mostly empty and echoes bounced back from closing the car doors. The scent of their pizza wasn't strong enough to overcome the stale oil and dusty concrete.

Carlos handed over the pizza box. "They want us in tech central."

"'Kay. I'm not sharing if the room's full."

"We're the ones on call. Don't know if they pulled anyone else in."

On the second floor, they by-passed their cubicles and went straight to the corner room filled with consoles and monitors. Two wall screens were playing videos from different public websites of the 'bigfoot' sightings. Captions running below the images detailed locations throughout the west where similar sightings were reported.

Sven set the pizza box on a side table, aligning it square with the edges. "Somebody left everything set up for us. Did that message say what we're looking at?"

Carlos grabbed a slice and sat facing the screens. "Someone's supposed to meet us here with instructions. Eat up before they get here."

"Don't worry about it," a voice said from behind him. "I just ate."

Carlos twisted around to put a name to the vaguely familiar voice. Ah. Iona. He turned back to the screens in case something new showed up there.

She stepped closer, "I can't guarantee Teal won't want any though."

"Teal?" Sven asked.

"Brand-new baby agent in training."

"I heard that," a new voice said. "But it's true and I'll accept any offerings of food."

Sven breathed out a soft whistle. "Gorgeous hair color."

Carlos turned back around. Teal's hair matched their name, a bright, intense shade over rosy cheeks and a slim, boyish frame. They wore a shiny silver catsuit with a belt around their hips and a holster-style bag.

Iona took a seat beside Carlos. She was dressed more casually in black exercise pants and a loose sweatshirt. "Teal, this is Sven and Carlos, field names Left and Right. Guys, this is Teal."

Teal bent their knees in a mini-curtsey. "No field name yet."

"May I suggest Peacock?" Sven said.

Teal snort-laughed. "My hair's not that shade of blue. Or green."

Carlos gestured to the screens. "Any chance your specialty is in computers, surveillance, or mind control?"

"Sorry," Teal shook their head. "Not yet anyway. But give me a few hours. I'm a quick study. I can learn anything the first time I read it and remember it for at least a few weeks. The tech team left me some reading material to study tonight." They cocked their head to one side. "Call me if anything interesting comes up. Or if you need help finishing that pizza."

After Teal was out of earshot, Carlos asked, "How new is she?"

"*They* started three weeks ago," Iona corrected. "An advantage of living on site is getting called in to help everyone working nights."

Sven plopped into a chair, "Anyone get around to telling them we wear regular clothes, not superhero costumes?"

Iona took the seat between them. "More times than they'd like to hear, apparently. Their regular clothes vary depending on their mood. Sometimes, it's a leather corset with chiffon, and sometimes it's a flannel shirt with suspenders and motorcycle boots."

"Okaaay," Carlos shook his head to clear the image Sven supplied of Teal in the outfits with swapped components – flannel and suspenders with chiffon and corset with the boots. "We're working now, right?"

Iona chuckled. "That's what we were told. The surveillance team reported scrambling at the Movement's headquarters. We're supposed to monitor all the Freedom Movement's sites and the news channels for any clues about what they're up to. And keep an eye on the effects of today's activities."

The monitors each showed four views with closed captioning. Websites and television channels. Most were still talking about the Bigfoot sightings.

"I take it they're letting the Bigfoot news out and suppressing the rest?" Carlos asked.

"That's the official word. Anything that looks legitimate gets blocked, but the rest we leave alone. All three of the phenos who were playing Bigfoot were taken to bureau lockup out of town. At least one is a shape-shifter."

Sven finished his slice of pizza. "Wish more of them were on our side."

Iona's lips pressed to a thin smile. "If all the amps were on our side, we would be out of jobs."

Sven chuckled. "They'll always find work for us. Just won't be what we're doing now."

Iona nodded acquiescence. "The forest fires don't seem to care about inter-amp politics."

"Speaking of..." Sven's voice trailed off as he indicated the wall monitors.

The caption below the newscaster read '... and the Vice President is scheduled to arrive next week to speak at the upcoming Nation Forestry Services Association Conference along with the governor.'

Sven turned from the screen towards Iona. "You invited to that? They should really be thanking the bureau agents who assist the firefighters."

She nodded, her eyes on the screen. "They thank us at an end of fire season thing every year. But if you're thinking more of us should be at this big meeting, that's a good way to get us an invite."

"You're reading her, right?" Carlos asked Sven. *"She is into you."*

"I spent all afternoon on a fake date with her. There's nothing there. No attraction at all." Sven answered mentally. "Write that up for Morrison and Manik. We're all in agreement that this is a likely target for Movement's next move?"

Iona blew out a breath. "If they're preparing something big that'll make the news, this is the most likely. Not the only possibility, but we're going to want a presence there. The VP will have Secret Service protection. They have to have amps on the team, right?"

"All the Secret Service field agents are amps," Carlos answered. "We looked into applying before we joined the bureau. *Check again. She's very interested in someone, and it's never me."* How could Sven miss all the clues? Iona's heart rate was slightly elevated, she kept glancing from them to the screens, never making eye contact for more than a moment, and every now and then, she wet her lips with the tip of her tongue.

"Why'd you join the bureau instead?"

Sven leaned back. *"You're misinterpreting. She could have anything on her mind.* They don't take mentals, especially not telepaths, for security. All the security details are staffed with amps, but they want enhanced sight and hearing mostly. Maybe some wind, water, magnetism, or electricity controllers. There's a few mentals – not telepaths – in the administrative and managerial positions."

Iona sniffed. "Sounds like discrimination."

Sven smiled. If Iona wasn't interested after one of his smiles, she never would be. "Ah, if only we were a protected class."

"There – did you notice her breath catch when you smiled?"

"You smiled too. It could be you. Or Teal, or someone she met yesterday."

"Okay," Iona said, flipping one screen of the nearest computer to email. "What warrants our concern and how many agents should we ask for?" She started typing before either of them answered.

Words filled the body of the email. None in the recipient line yet. She included the official visit date, the size of the convention hall, the possibility of having firefighter bureau agents invited, the Vice President's likely arrival and departure route, and the most likely hotels where the governor would stay. "Can you guys contact surveillance – it's Bark tonight, I think – and ask for any details he's heard that might prove this as a likely target?

Sven flashed him a quick smile. *"Wonder twin powers activate."*

"Do you have to say that every time?"

"It's my catchphrase."

"It's not a catchphrase if I'm the only one who hears it."

They slid their minds together. Literally easier to do it than think about doing it. Or explaining it to anyone else. Just think about merging and in half a second, their thoughts were shared. And sharing more than doubled the strength of their telepathy, telekinetics, and tele-whatever else they needed.

"Bark?" Sven took the lead. He was always the more talkative of them. *"We're working on a lead here after you reported something being planned out there."*

"Left and Right?" Bark thought back at them. Some agents were better than others are replying to telepaths. He wasn't bad, but you could feel the strain he put into focusing his thoughts at them.

"Yeah. They called us in after you reported activity at the headquarters. We're wondering if it has anything to do with the Vice President and Governor speaking at a conference this weekend."

"Let me see if I can get closer. This pine is great for camouflage, but not close enough to hear anything."

"Don't put yourself at risk of discovery."

"Number one rule, man. Er, men."

Sven flashed a smile, almost a smirk, at Carlos. Iona caught sight of it. "What? You guys telling jokes over there?"

Carlos shrugged. "I wouldn't exactly call it a joke. A play on words. He's trying to see if getting closer will help."

Carlos closed his connection to keep Bark from hearing. *"Her smile is pretty great, too."* Iona was tweaking the email she still hadn't addressed. She'd opened more windows with details on the conference and speakers.

"I'm beginning to think you like her."

"As if women are ever interested in me. That's your department."

Sven made another noise aloud. Kind of a 'pah' that made Iona look over again and shake her head. *"I get their attention, but none of them stick around for a relationship. Perks of this powerset."*

"Bonded telepaths have never been common? Shit. You mean all your girlfriends left because of me, didn't they?"

"Guys?" Bark said, still carefully focusing his thoughts. *"I'm closer now. The dozen or so who arrived in the past hour are all together in the main room. I can't hear them, but it sure looks like a planning session. They have charts and maps and laptops."*

"Take any pictures you can and get back to a safer place as fast as possible. We'll do some research and see if there are any other attractive targets coming up."

If big targets were Freedom's objective. *"Today's events weren't attached to anything in particular,"* Carlos said.

"Yeah, I know," Sven answered. *"But this is big enough to attract their attention. We'll definitely look at other things, too. For all we know, they're planning a birthday party."*

Bark's focus was almost painful to feel. He tried so hard. *"Birthday parties don't usually have this much logistics involved. They're tracing routes on a map and it looks like they're assigning spotters on the major highways."* Trying to explain that he could relax and just think at them naturally never worked in the past.

Sven nodded, though Bark wouldn't be able to tell. *"You're right, this conference is the mostly likely thing. We'll check out other newsworthy events coming up, just in case. Even getting on air during a basketball or hockey game would get them some press."*

"I'm back at my pine tree now." Bark might be getting tired. Or relaxing. Either way, there wasn't as much strain in his thoughts. *"If they mess with the playoffs, there'll be a ton of pissed-off fans."*

Sven made eye contact with Carlos. *"Keep monitoring them. We'll send a report upstream and see where they want us to focus."*

Iona sat back from the keyboard, arms folded across her chest. She'd added Morrison's and Manik's names to the send field in the email still displayed on the wall screen. "If you're done, take a look at this and tell me what else I need to add."

She'd included details about the forestry conference, names of bureau agents who'd fought forest fires last season, a rating of the potential threat level, and the likelihood that this was the next target.

"Looks good to me. Add Gator too, since she's leading with Manik," Carlos said. *"We still need to talk about this."*

"What this?" Sven projected an air of confusion, but tipped his chair back and grinned lazily at Iona. "Send it."

"Have women broken up with you because of me?"

Sven's face stayed neutral. "Wait, ask them how long they want us to hang out here tonight and whether we can come in late tomorrow."

Iona sent the email. "Too late. You'll have to send those questions yourself."

"She's certainly more relaxed around me than she was this afternoon. Must be your influence."

"You didn't answer the question."

Sven pulled a keyboard close and opened and email window. *"Fine. Okay. Most of my breakups were over the job. Hours too long, schedule too unpredictable, worry that I was putting myself into danger. You know."*

Carlos nodded and watched words appear on the screen where Sven typed. *"Most?"*

"A few of them freaked out when they realized that you knew everything I was doing, or thinking, or feeling."

"You didn't explain it well then."

Sven sent the email. "Now we just have to wait around for an answer. Or for something else to blow up."

Iona shrugged "There's a regular night shift for the worst of that. We're just back-up."

"They were amps, but not mentals and not with the bureau. I don't think they wanted to understand. I wasn't worth the extra effort."

"And this was after they'd seen you?"

"Ha Ha. Looks aren't everything and I'm not everyone's type." Sven didn't look her way, but sent a brief image of Iona.

"Don't be so sure." Carlos stood and stretched. "Anyone want more soda?" He refilled his glass and poured a half cup for Iona. *"You're leaving something out."*

"Fine. One woman. Don't know if you'll remember her. Fran."

Carlos sent back a faintly-remembered image, blurry around the edges, of a bright smile and tousled black curls.

"Yeah. Her. She was jealous of you. She couldn't handle the idea that I'd always be closer to you than to a girlfriend."

"So, not only do I have no romantic prospects, I'm ruining yours."

"There are always prospects. It's getting them to pan out where we run into problems."

Iona stretched out her legs, then tucked them under her butt. Not quite cross-legged, but vaguely yoga-like. "I'm surprised how restful it is with the two of you here. No chatter, just quiet and peaceful."

Sven laughed. "We can be loud if you'd like." He looked at Carlos. "Has anyone ever called me 'quiet' before?"

"Not that I can recall. Goofy maybe. Inattentive, smart-ass. Oh yeah, Morrison prefers smart-ass."

She tilted her head, that red hair catching the light. "Sorry I said anything." Her smile was sweet though.

Carlos answered her smile. "We do get stuck in our own conversations. Sorry we left you out." And her interruption gave him time to think about this. How should he apologize? What could he do to keep from messing up Sven's future relationships?

"No worries. Quiet is good sometimes. Daytimes down in the labs are never quiet."

"With Doc Choi always scurrying around?" Sven said. "She still trying to plot out the best matches to produce the next generation of amps?"

"Oh yeah. She has lists and books of lists. If nature doesn't take its course, she's not above coercing us into sperm or egg donation."

Carlos shrugged. "I wouldn't be here otherwise. Mom needed to have her priest confirm that artificial insemination wasn't the same as adultery first."

"Same here." Iona gave a short nod that didn't give away her thoughts. "Except for the priest. The bureau was pushing her to have a kid or six but she hadn't met Dad yet. My sister and I have different donors. Our brother was born after they got married." She glanced at Sven.

Sven shook his head. "My folks were already sweethearts when the bureau recruited them from the old country."

A chirp from the computer drew their attention to the wall screen. Manik's reply to their email. Iona opened it just as another chirp announced Morrison's response. She opened them side-by-side.

Sven laughed. "Figures. Two bosses never can agree."

Morrison's message was to pack it in for the night and reconvene in the morning with the whole task force. Manik wanted them to collect more data from the Movement's HQ and write a detailed report.

"I'll be here all night," Iona said. "We can split it up – you two pack it in and I'll hunt for more data. Teal's on night shift and we can contact the rest of their team if we need more help."

Carlos still watched the screen. "They copied each other on their replies. Wait a few to see how they resolve it."

The quick patter of footsteps wove through the cubicles until a slightly out of breath Teal appeared. "Iona, Roth is asking for you."

Iona stood so fast that Carlos had to catch her chair before it spun into the desk. "You're not supposed to go near him."

Teal shook their hair back. "I didn't. He shouted and security called me on the intercom."

"I better see what he wants now. Who wants to be my backup?"

Carlos glanced at Sven to give him first choice.

"Go. I'll wait for the big guns to come to agreement."

Carlos stood. "I'll take in-person backup and he'll help from here."

Iona gave him an accepting nod and strode off. He hustled to catch up, the murmur of Sven and Teal in soft discussion behind them. She did hold the elevator for him. He grinned his thanks but tried not to hold eye contact. People were wary of telepaths getting too familiar.

Iona pressed the button for the infirmary level and the doors slid closed. "What's your gut feeling on all this," she asked, leaning against the wall. "Full disclosure and the Movement."

"That could be a trick question."

"Not meant to be."

"Well then, I agree with some of their proposals. Full disclosure was always supposed to happen, but we have to be very careful how we go about it. The Movement's everything-right-now demands will make some things very much worse." The floor counter reached the first basement level and the elevator settled to a stop. "Phenos might have it easier, but telepaths in the open? No one's going to trust us. And you'll never get fire insurance." He waited for her to lead the way as the doors slid open.

"Good answer. You've thought this through." They passed the infirmary reception desk, unstaffed this time of night. Their footsteps echoed down the corridor lined with treatment rooms to one side and doctors' offices to the other.

"Who hasn't?"

"I've met a few." Iona turned past the last treatment room, before they reached the longer-term patient rooms. Her room was probably down there. A metal double door barred their way. She tapped in a code on the keypad on the wall, a green LED flashed twice and she pressed the door open just wide enough for them to slip through.

"Who's Roth?"

"He's a Firestarter they brought in. Was a Movement member. Lit up a house with an agent inside and Lisa risked her life to get him out. They grabbed Roth later and brought him here. The doc and others have me talking to him now and again to see if we can rehabilitate him."

A guard station just beyond the doors was staffed by a single pale man dividing his attention between them and a small bank of surveillance monitors. Four panels switched views between corridors, empty cells, occupied cells, and outer doors. More were empty. One showed a dark haired man in loose-fitting pants, tank top and slippers.

"That him?"

She nodded, eyes on the screen. "Hi Bruce. I got word that our guest wanted to talk to me."

Bruce nodded and jerked one hand towards the corridor beyond his station. "Go on ahead. You know the way." He handed her a key with a card attached.

She reached over the desk and pressed a switch on the console. "Roth, Iona here. I heard you wanted to talk to me."

On the screen, the guy stopped pacing and looked at the camera. "Yeah." His voice was only a little distorted by the speakers. "Can you come to my door?"

"Give me a minute or two." She released the switch.

Iona thanked Bruce and led Carlos down an industrial grey hallway lined with doors distinguishable only by small number placards at the top of the frame. A few small signs bearing bureau slogans and regularly spaced red fire extinguishers broke up the grey expanse.

"Is he rehabilitatable?"

"Not sure yet. Not my area of training anyway." She stopped beside one of the fire extinguishers. "Come with me, but stay back, out of his sight. He's usually cooperative, but with all that's been going on, I don't trust him around others."

"He's been locked up for what, a month or so now? Are they letting him have contact with the Movement?"

"'Letting'? No." She shook her head. "They have telepaths, too. If you ever come up with a way to reliably block telepaths, be sure to let someone know."

Carlos's face warmed and he studied his hands. That should have been his first thought. "I think I'm just glad *we* can't be blocked."

"Oh, me too. But times like this it might be nice. Or at least to have one mental who can block out an area when we need them to."

"Huh. That's something Sven and I haven't ever tried. Individually, we're not much, but together we're more than an average telepath."

"You both seem more than *not much* to me." Iona slowed long enough to flash a grin his way. "All these cells have multiple locks so no single amp can open them from the inside. The walls are fireproof, freezeproof, wind resistant, waterproof, and resistant to any other amp power they could think of. There's a little window in the door I can open to talk face-to-face, that's the weak point in the cell."

"And I just hide off to the side in case you need me to call for help or something?"

"Or something. Off to the side and behind me."

They stopped by a door that looked no different from any of the others. Carlos continued past Iona and stood between her and the opposite wall of the corridor. Her ponytail swung and she turned her head and studied him. She shook her head and used it to gesture to her other side, back the way they'd come.

He sidestepped back until she gave an approving nod. She pressed one finger against her lips, stepped to the door, and rapped twice.

"Roth? I'm here. Give me time to get this open."

A noise from beyond the door might have been an acknowledgement. Or a belch. Or a chair scraping against the floor. It was hard to tell. Iona used a keycard, a key, and a passcode on the three different locks to open the window in the door. A face with indeterminate skin tone and brown eyes under bushy dark brows peered out.

"That didn't take long," he said, his voice husky.

"I was in the building. What do you need?"

He snort-laughed. "Out of here."

Iona shrugged. "You know I can't do that."

"Really. I need to be out tonight."

"And I'm not authorized. I don't have any way to open your door even if I were."

It looked like Roth slumped against the door. "Can you get someone else? How high up do they have to be?"

"A few levels above me. I'm just a grunt around here."

"Then I'll need a way to get them here." His face disappeared from the window and a stream of fire shot out. Carlos jumped back but Iona stepped towards it with her palms to the fire. No other way to describe it, she *caught* the fire in both hands and pressed the stream into a sphere. Beads of sweat on her forehead ran together and made trails down her temples and nose. Her hands shook as she compressed the fire from basketball-sized, to softball-sized, and finally to golf ball-sized.

"Link now. Need power."

Sven opened his mind fully and Carlos used their combined might to push the window closed. Without any of the keys they couldn't lock it, but he held it pressed against the door while Iona rolled the ball of fire back and forth.

Sulphur and charcoal filled the air, like the end of a night of fireworks around a campfire. Roth pounded on his side of the door, then yelped when a whoosh sounded within.

Iona's lips curled up weakly. "He forgot about the fire suppression foam. His first blast was close enough that the sensors didn't read it as inside his cell."

"Are you okay?"

She nodded, stray hairs stuck to her face with sweat, the rest of her ponytail limp along her back. "Thanks for closing that."

"Can you lock it before we run out of kinetic power?"

"Yeah. Think so." She transferred the fireball to one palm and stepped to the door. Keylock, passcode, key; she locked all of them.

Carlos released the hold against the door and relaxed his connection with Sven. *"Thanks. We've got it now."*

"Fill me in when you can."

"Sure. Did you know she could do that? It was amazing. She's amazing."

Sven just answered with a wave of confusion instead of words.

"He shot a bolt of fire at us and she caught it in her hands like it was nothing."

Iona cleared her throat. "Do you think you could grab that fire extinguisher back there?"

"Yeah. For your hands?" *Stupid, so busy being impressed I didn't think about her getting hurt.*

She nodded at the wall behind them. "No, some of it got past me and the sign is burning."

Crap. Smoldering more than flaming, but he should have been more aware. He ran back to an extinguisher, wrenched it from the wall, and hurried back with the base of it banging against his thighs with every step.

Iona still held the little ball of fire. So Carlos yanked the pin from the handle, aimed the nozzle at the charred ring spouting smoke in center of the sign and pulled the trigger. A blast of white powder coated the sign and the dark smoke faded away.

"There are sprinklers in the cells, but not the hallway?"

Iona shrugged. "They hoped that anyone using flames out here would be a bureau agent."

"Fair enough." He hauled the extinguisher back to its bracket. "Okay to keep this in use? I didn't empty it."

"For tonight at least. Paperwork before we're done for the night." Iona stared at the ball of fire in her hand. "Hang onto it for a minute, I wanna try something." She extended both hands, the one with Roth's fire and the empty one. A tiny flame sprang up in the empty hand, a brighter golden yellow than the compressed one from Roth. Iona stared at it and it moved, spiraling out from the middle of her palm, then running up each finger in turn.

"Be ready now," she warned, moving her attention to the other hand. The ball of fire glowed brighter, a deep, angry orange-red. It rocked from side to side. She brought her hands together and poured her flame beside the ball. The flame circled the ball once, then moved towards it. The ball rocked to the side of her hand and she cupped them together. Her flame moved faster and hit the ball. A fiery bolt shot to the ceiling. Iona leaned back, narrowly missing getting hit in the face.

"Is that what you expected?" Carlos squeezed off a shot of fire suppressant where a circle of fire burned on the ceiling. Drips fell back onto the floor, and them.

Iona shook out her hands. "I didn't know *that* would happen. I don't play with other people's fire much."

Carlos tucked the fire extinguisher nozzle against the canister and brushed white powder from his hair. "Good thing you're fireproof."

She shook her head with a short laugh. "I wish. *My* fire won't burn me. I have to focus on any other fire and make it mine. If I'm not paying attention, I'm as flammable as the next person." She ducked as more residue fell from the ceiling and used the back of her hand to brush some from Carlos's arm. "We should get washed up. It's not toxic, but gets irritating if it stays on your skin for too long."

"Good idea. What about the mess?" He swung the fire extinguisher to indicate the powder on the wall, ceiling, and floor.

Iona exhaled a long, deep sigh. "I'll add a custodial request to my reports for tonight. Let's go."

Carlos walked at her side, pausing only to put the extinguisher back on its hook. He easily matched her stride, even though she had two or three inches on him. One sideways glance made him think she was slowing her pace for him.

At the end of the detainment corridor, Iona nodded to Bruce. "We need to wash up. Could you call custodial? There's some fire extinguisher residue back there."

Bruce grunted and started typing on his computer.

Iona led Carlos behind Bruce's chair. "In here." She opened a door that blended with the paneling. Inside was a small bathroom. "Lean over the sink and brush it all out of your hair before washing."

He did as he was told while she waited in the doorway. Loose, dried powder fell out first. One breath of the acrid odor and he held his breath until he was done brushing it out. He scrubbed at his arms where a few blobs of the foam had landed.

"Good." Iona stepped up behind him, letting the door close with a soft click. "Hand me a wet paper towel so I can check your neck."

He followed instructions and stood facing the sink and mirror. At his back, Iona tugged his collar down and wiped from right to left. Her touch was light. A shiver rippled down his back, not tickling really, but some part of him responded electrically.

Iona didn't seem to notice his reaction. She stretched up to look at the top of his head. He watched her reflection in the mirror, but her eyes stayed on his scalp. "Bend your head forward and close your eyes."

Her fingers ran through his hair, light pressure against his scalp leaving tingling trails behind. Better than a shampoo at the fancy stylist place Sven dragged him to.

"When you get back here, you have to see this video Teal found that the Movement posted. The vid claims it's showing a weather amp in action, blowing clouds around, but it's got camera shake and half in the dark. Looks like

a bad student film." Sven included a brief view of the video.

It was so bad.

"What's so funny?"

"Sven showed me a clip they found on the Movement's site. It's not all that ridiculous, but he made it seem like it was."

Her fingers stilled. "You two are always in contact, aren't you? You see the same things?"

"Not exactly."

She ran her fingers up through his hair, probably making the curls all fluffed up and stupid-looking, and removed her hand from his head.

He opened his eyes and looked at her mirrored reflection. Her gaze was focused off to the side. "It's more internal. I feel every emotion he feels and vice versa. We can chat anytime – just like we're in the same room. If we want to share something we saw or heard, we can, but it's a deliberate thing, it doesn't just happen." He turned around and made eye contact. "Telepaths might be the most misunderstood amps. It doesn't help that everyone's power has different ranges and limitations."

That produced a small smile from Iona. "The fire isn't that hard to explain after all. Make fire, shoot fire. Probably interferes with relationships just as much."

He blew out a breath. "More than I knew. Can I ask your opinion? As a woman?"

She stepped back. "I don't speak for all women."

Open mouth, insert foot.

"What'd you do now?"

"Talked without thinking. Never mind."

"Sorry. One non-telepathic person's opinion would help me out."

"Okay then."

Suddenly, the washroom was way too confining. "Do you still need to wash your hands?"

She looked at her hands and arms. "Good idea. Switch places."

They turned around each other, front-to-front. The room was way too small to avoid all contact. It was nice contact, but not the kind of contact you wanted with someone you were just starting to know better.

"Go ahead." She soaped her hands and scrubbed them together. "What's the question?"

"Would you feel awkward dating someone with the bond Sven and I have? Apparently it's caused problems for him before."

"Just for him? Not for you?" Iona turned off the faucet and tore a paper towel from the dispenser.

"He's had more girlfriends than me."

She shrugged and made a non-committal hum. "Well, I can see where some women might be concerned. Wondering if their secrets were being shared, even unintentionally. Or being jealous that the two of you are closer to each other than to them."

Carlos nodded. "He said both have happened. What can I do about it? I don't want to keep him from finding someone."

"Do you really know what each other is feeling? Just emotionally? Or physically, too?"

"Both. Um… tickle me."

Her eyebrows quirked up. "What?"

"I'm not ticklish, but he is."

She put her fingertips against his sides, right above his hipbones and wiggled them. Her touch was softly therapeutic. Mom was right about his needing more physical contact in his life.

"Gaah! What are you doing?"

"Oh, did I bother you? Sorry."

He grinned at Iona. "Got him. That never gets old."

"You two must have been terrors in school."

"Mostly to each other. Our link came in handy for tests. He's better at dates, names, and formulas. I'm better at theories, conclusions, and reasons."

"Are you two heading back any time soon?"

"We should get going. I think he's waiting for us. Would it make a difference for a relationship that we share feelings?"

She pulled the door open. "It might. Especially for intimate situations."

"Just what I was afraid of. That isn't something we can just fix."

"It's too bad you're not both gay."

"Huh?" It didn't sound like she intended it as a joke.

"Knowing what each other is feeling? The sex would be amazing."

Carlos's cheeks burned. Great, there wasn't a solution to this problem and now whenever Sven kissed someone, Carlos had to wonder whether the warm tingly feeling he got was a reflection of Sven's emotions or because of his own attraction to Sven.

CHAPTER FIVE

Iona led the way into the elevator back to the second floor. Carlos was adorable when he was embarrassed. She'd meant to be honest, but it was a little mean. Fun, but mean. Maybe his payback for getting her to tickle Sven through him?

When the floor readout pinged their arrival, Carlos pressed the 'hold' button. "Um…"

She waited.

"Don't tell Sven I'm saying this, but if your fake date picnic today went well enough that you'd want to try it for real, I think he likes you and would like to have a for-real date."

Carlos thought Sven thought their 'date' was worth repeating. Which one of them was deluding themselves? She shook her head. The picnic she was on didn't have any sparks between them. A few flames, but no sparks. No chemistry that she felt.

She must have waited too long before answering, because he asked, "What? Don't you like him? Everyone likes him."

"Not that. He's great. I'm just too messed up." Too messed up to feel anything, to recognize a good thing when it's right in front of her. "Don't tell him I said that, please. I don't know exactly what my problem is, but it's probably going to take a while."

He released the hold on the door. "For what it's worth, you two are gorgeous together."

The doors slid open. "Thanks? That's not really necessary for a relationship, you know. Let's go see what mister gorgeous wants."

The elevator vestibule was quiet, but well-lit. Once they entered the cubicle floor, conversation from the tech corner was just audible, but indistinct.

Sven stood up and turned their way. "It's about time. Teal got through."

Iona walked faster, weaving through the maze of cubicles. "Through? Into the Movement's files?"

"Yep." Teal popped to their feet, just the brightly-colored hair visible above the cubicle walls. "I got through their firewall and copied all their files over."

Iona reached them and leaned against a desk. Carlos was close behind and dropped into a chair at her side.

"And," Sven continued, "Morrison reviewed your report and gave a soft approval on your plan. Pending whatever else this one discovers." He indicated Teal with a jerk of his head. "He'll send in a request to get you and some of the other forest fire crew admitted to the conference. Otherwise, we're off for the night. Briefing at ten tomorrow."

Teal made a strained gurgling sound from deep within their chest. "Ten. And I'm expected to be there, even if I'm tracing their web activity all night." Their shoulders slumped and they drew a hand across their brow dramatically. "My life is so hard." Then a shrug, a grin and, "Thanks for the pizza, nice to meet you, and I'll see you in the morning. Goodnight." They left the tech bullpen with a wave.

Iona chuckled. "Teal keeps things lighter around here."

Sven leaned down to the keyboard and closed most of the windows. "And more colorful. Can't wait to see what Gator makes of them."

"Gator's actually amused. Morrison, not so much, but he's warming up."

Carlos stood and pushed in chairs. "I'll take care of the dinner things, then we can go." He gathered pizza-related debris and the empty cola bottle and left the area.

Sven watched Carlos leave. "You know," he said softly. "He's very impressed with you. With your control down there. I think he might, you know, like you. He's too shy to ever ask a woman out, but if you wanted to ask him out some time, I'm sure he'd accept." He looked around. Carlos was still well out of earshot. "Don't tell him I said anything."

"Oh, I won't."

"What? Don't you like him?"

"He's great. I like him. Both of you. But, like I told you, I've had problems lately and don't think I'm ready to date at all right now."

Sven flashed a smile, all cheer and teeth. "Just keep him in mind whenever you decide you're ready."

"It's good to see you two have each other's backs."

"Yeah, we're all about the teamwork."

"Dishes are done. You ready to head home?" Carlos called as he came within view.

"Sure." Sven turned to Iona. "Are you done for the night, too?"

She rolled her shoulders. "Hope so. We don't have to pay for board or checkups in the infirmary, but being available for every little thing cuts into any downtime. I'll take the elevator down with you guys. Teal will call me if anything comes up."

The aisles between cubicles were too narrow for three abreast, so Iona walked behind the guys. Sven might get more attention with his height, broad shoulders, and tousled blond hair, but Carlos wasn't hard on the eyes either. Glossy black curls just past his collar, slim hips, and ramrod-straight posture. If she could get past the embarrassment of thinking that he knew what Sven knew about the mini helper in her purse, and of course, get over whatever was keeping her from wanting sex with any man, he wouldn't be a bad choice.

Maybe that potential embarrassment wasn't something she really needed to worry about, given the other conversations she'd had with them. If they each thought the other was interested in her, what did that say about their ability to read each other? Or they really both were interested, but in the name of friendship were letting the other have the first chance to ask her out.

So, I'm a prize now? Pfft. In my own mind, maybe. Not such a prize if I'm afraid to touch anyone passionately. Which wasn't the fault of either of them.

Sven tripped and fumbled to keep on his feet. Iona was close enough to crash into his back. His well-muscled back. She bumped him hard enough to rebound sideways and clip Carlos's shoulder with her own. He got his arm around her waist in time to keep her from rattling any cubicle walls.

"Thanks." That wasn't enough exertion, or excitement, to have made her heart rate increase. Either she was more tired than she thought, or she really needed to work out more.

Sven glanced back. "Sorry about that." His eyes were downcast, but those dimples hinted at his amusement at something.

Carlos eased his hand from her side, but kept his palm against her back. For support? "Those big feet of his get in the way a lot."

"New shoes." Sven pointed. "Still breaking them in."

The sneakers he wore had long since lost the luster of un-sullied footwear. No brilliant white glow that screamed 'fresh from the box'. Iona raised an eyebrow at the scuffs he displayed.

Sven chuckled. "Okay. I'm just tired. Let's go home."

They reached the elevators with no further incidents and the doors slid open immediately after Sven hit the call button. Each of them took a corner – Iona and Carlos in the back and Sven beside the bank of floor buttons. He pressed two – infirmary level and parking level – and looked to Iona. "Right?"

"Yep." She stifled a yawn and leaned against the woodgrain paneling. It wasn't past her bedtime yet, but getting pretty darn close.

Both men smiled at exactly the same time, the exact same amount of smile – the soft curve of their lips and twinkle in their eyes like they'd shared a private joke.

"What?" *Telepaths*.

"Nothing." Carlos looked at his feet.

"Told you," Sven said at the exact same time. He met Iona's gaze and flashed a bright smile. "He was making fun of my shoes. But look at what's on his feet."

She hadn't paid any attention to his shoes before. She bent forward and Carlos pulled a pant leg to expose his ankle and show off his woven leather sandals.

"Those are nice. I have a pair like that." The elevator doors slid open and she gave them each a smile. "Goodnight. Don't forget to write up something about Roth tonight. I'll copy you on my report."

"Will do," Carlos answered.

One of Doc Choi's assistants sat at the infirmary station, intent on the screen before him. "I'm heading in for the night, Andre," Iona said well before she reached him. She'd promised to keep from startling him again when he was that focused.

"Hey, Iona." He didn't look up. "Bruce said there was some action on his wing. Are you writing a report?"

"As soon as I get to my room."

"Copy me on it. Boss has me updating Roth's activities daily."

"You got it. Goodnight."

Back in her room, she locked the door and kicked off her shoes. The quick report form should be enough. The basics were easy enough. Under 'additional details', she noted the potential plot they'd uncovered and the need for corridor cleanup. File saved and sent to the task force, to Carlos, to the doc, and to Andre.

Iona shut off the computer and sat on the floor for her night-time stretching routine. Some nights she wished that could be all, but the doc wanted her using her vibrator morning and night and any time her day ran long enough to be eighteen hours between orgasms.

After a quick wash she settled in her bed wearing an old t-shirt. She pulled the full-sized toy from its box and turned it in her hands. It had every possible setting. Several she hadn't tried yet.

Experimenting wasn't on her mind tonight. Just a quick get-it-over-with and get some sleep. Thumbing the on switch with one hand, she ran the other over her body, imaging that same set of anonymous hands from the afternoon. They stroked her thighs, feather-light touch sending tingles up her center, then up to circle her breasts one at a time, beading her nipples to taut points. Back to her thighs, but tipped to glide the tips of the nails over the sensitive skin there.

She arched her back and slid the vibrator between her legs. An unintended moan escaped. Anonymous hands were the best kind. All imaginary, no strings attached, no fragile, fleshy body to burn up. No. Do not think about fire now. Follow the hand softly stroking the most responsive places. Ripples of pleasure trailed after the touch. Concentrate on the vibrations purring against her clitoris inside and out. Rock hips in time with the motion.

Faster and faster until she reached climax. As the waves rolled out from her center, her mind focused on two images. A sweet, warm smile and a pair of blue eyes with a delightful twinkle. She switched off the vibrator and let her head sink into her pillow. "All right, brain. Do we need to have a talk? Certain faces are strictly off-limits here.'

Fellow agents, no matter how charming or gorgeous, are not on the menu. She wiped off and boxed the vibrator and curled onto her side to sleep. Besides, there was no chemistry between them. None at all.

The last thing she remembered before falling asleep was the image of that smile and those eyes.

CHAPTER SIX

Sven groaned and swore at his alarm. The meeting wasn't until ten. He swatted at the bedside table, hitting the clock several times, but the alarm still rang. Another swat at the table and his phone clattered off the charging station. He rubbed his eyes and snatched it up.

"What? Meeting's not 'til ten. And why didn't you just shout?"

"Sorry," Carlos said. "Change of plans. They want me in to add to last night's report. And I did shout. You were sleeping the sleep of the dead."

Sven sat up and swung his legs over the side. "Half the night maybe. If we're going in now, you're buying the coffee."

"Okay. I'm making toast now too."

"Don't hurry." Sven tapped the connection closed. Stupid meeting. Stupid reports. He flung the blankets off with enough force to impress anyone watching with his commitment to rising. Getting his body up took more time. He finally swung his legs over the side of the bed and scrubbed at his face with both hands. Meetings today.

That meant shower, shave, khakis and a button-down shirt.

Whatever had him tossing and turning all night left him moving at half speed. When Carlos knocked, Sven was still buttoning his dark blue shirt. Maybe bringing out the color in his eyes would distract from the dark circles underneath them. One glance in the mirror by the door told him that the shirt wasn't nearly enough. Dark glasses were his only salvation.

"Didn't I give you a key?" he asked after unlocking the door.

Carlos stood on the landing, his smile way too perky for the hour. "Sorry, my hands are full." For proof, he held up two travel mugs and two paper bags. "Coffee and breakfast."

"You're still buying me another." He took the mug from the near hand.

"Got it." Carlos followed him into the apartment and pushed the door closed. "Do you need much longer? Carlos was also dressed for meetings. Charcoal slacks and a black-and-grey patterned shirt.

Sven sipped from the travel mug. Coffee with vanilla caramel creamer. "Nah. I think shoes are all I'm missing." Two more sips while he found the shoes that went with the slacks. Phone and keys and he was ready to go. He lifted the mug towards Carlos. "Thanks. I'm really glad I gave you that coffee maker for Christmas." They headed down to the car parked street-side.

"The least I could do for making you get up early and drive me."

"And you're buying me another coffee when we get there." He unlocked the doors and they settled into their seats.

"Of course." Carlos's smile was both sweet and ingratiating.

"What's in the breakfast bags?"

"A banana and an English muffin with peanut butter. Want it now?"

The engine purred to life and Sven put the car in gear. "Sure. Hand me the English muffin."

They ate in silence for a few blocks. Carlos folded his banana peel and tucked it back in the paper bag. "Did we share dreams again last night?"

"I think so. She was in it, wasn't she?"

"Yeah. I mean, I didn't see her face, but knew it was her."

"Dreams are like that."

"But we don't usually share about the same person."

Sven licked peanut butter off his finger. "We did spend a lot of time with her yesterday. Both of us. And you had a dramatic event with her."

"More amazingly cool than dramatic, but yeah." Carlos took a long drink of his coffee. "She said something about us, though."

"Banana."

"Not that."

Sven snorted. "I'll take the banana now."

"Oh." Carlos passed it over.

"You going to tell me?"

Carlos sighed. "Sure. She said that if we were gay, we'd have amazing sex."

Sven snorted. "How did that even come up?" A side glance showed a blush on Carlos's cheeks that matched the embarrassment that poured off his mind.

"She was asking how our power works."

Sven eased the car to a stop at light. Just a few blocks to the bureau. "Still quite the segue."

"It was about how we share feelings."

He glanced over at Carlos again. "She's not wrong."

"Something you've thought about?"

The light turned green. "Not so much. I mean, you're hot and all, but not my type. You know, the best sex is about the emotions behind everything. Knowing how your partner feels and reacting to it would make it the best."

"I guess." Carlos was staring out the window. "I never thought about using our powers that way."

"Me either. But it's something." He pulled the car into the garage entrance.

They rode the elevator to the first floor where Sven led the way to the coffee kiosk. "I'll have a double espresso with a shot of hazelnut."

"On top of the mug you already drank?" Carlos shook his head, but placed the order along with a green tea for himself.

Sven grasped the steaming paper cup. "Ah, elixir of life." He sipped it steadily until the elevator came.

They rode the elevator up one floor to the realm of cubicles and conference rooms. "Thanks for coming in early. See you at the ten o'clock."

"I'm going to clean out my inbox while you're meeting. Call me if it's boring and you need some delightful conversation."

"Always."

They parted ways at the first intersection – Carlos to a conference room and Sven to his cube. His desktop was clear, just keyboard, mouse, and yesterday's coffee mug in need of washing. He scooted it back to make room for the fresh cup and logged on. Email triage engaged. Delete, delete, delete. Sort to folders. Didn't take long enough, then he had to actually read and respond to messages. He made it through four.

"Hey. How's the meeting going?"

"So far so good, I guess. Going over what happened last night so the guys in charge can decide whether to keep Roth here or send him to a more secure facility."

"Who all's there?"

"Me and Iona, Morrison, Manik, and Gator as heads of the task force, Choi because she's studying him, and Cameron Reyes from Bureau security."

"How's Iona this morning?"

"She seems fine. You haven't finished your email yet, have you?"

"Sorted most of it."

"I have to report now. Get to work."

Sven turned back to his computer. More reports read and filed. Some emails answered—one to his mom even—and two bureau employee surveys completed. Most of the surrounding cubicles were filling with people arriving for the day and Sven's coffee cup was nearly empty. He rocked back from his desk and finished the espresso. He looked from his empty cup, to the computer monitor, to yesterday's mug. Washing out that mug seemed the best use of his time right now.

With an empty cup in each hand, one paper and one ceramic, he wove through the maze of cubicles to the break room near the center where he could wash one cup and dispose of the other. Broadcast was there, heating water for the special tea blend he brought from home. They exchanged greetings but Cast didn't act awake enough for a longer conversation just yet.

"How's the meeting going now?" he asked Carlos as he returned to his cube.

"We've given all our reports, now the heads are arguing over what to do with him. Done with your email yet?"

"Sort of."

"You've got time before the ten o'clock. They can't start that until we're done here."

"It going to run late?"

"Not sure yet. Security and Morrison want the guy moved, but Choi's not done with him here."

Sven settled back in his cube and stared down the rest of his email. Last night's dream nudged his conscious mind again. He hadn't been sure it was Iona at the time, but now that Carlos confirmed it, it was clear. *"How's Iona this morning?"*

"Still seems fine. Oh, we're wrapping up now. No decision yet, but they'll meet again later to sort it out. Iona and I don't need to be there though. See you in the big meeting room in a few."

Just enough time to take his freshly washed mug downstairs and get it filled with coffee. He'd be fully caffeinated and could enjoy Carlos's reaction.

The conference room table was half-filled with task force members when he made it back upstairs. He sat beside Iona and across from Carlos with a hearty greeting.

She looked at his still-full mug with a sigh. "I should've gotten some."

A sudden surge of generosity hit him. "Want it? My lips haven't touched it yet."

Her eyes brightened. There were golden glints in the brown depths he hadn't noticed yesterday. "Really?"

He slid it over. "I've had two already."

"Softy."

"Like you didn't send me a nudge to do that."

Teal flounced in, still in last night's silver suit, but with a purple cardigan covering their arms and shoulders. They yawned and took the open set at the foot of the table between Sven and Carlos.

They pressed their lips into a thin smile. "At least my shift is at an end. I have a very comfortable bed waiting for me after this meeting."

Morrison, Manik, and Gator were the last to arrive. They took positions at the head of the table. "Everyone here?" Manik asked.

Morrison grunted. "Let's get started."

He caught the task force up on their late-night breakthroughs. Not much about Iona and Carlos's encounter with the prisoner, but mostly about Teal's hacked-for data and what it meant for the team moving forward. "So, for today, I want the surveillance team on the Movement every minute. Report in every time one of them leaves the house, every time two of them talk to each other, and every time one of them touches any device connected to the internet. The tech team will be monitoring all their known sites, searching for any new posts anywhere, and tracking down any leads on this conference. Flame, since yesterday, there's a drastic increase in the number of posts on Movement sites that mention fire-powered amps. Nothing that calls you out, but looks like they're stirring things up. Watch yourself extra carefully out in the field."

Sven could only see Iona in profile, but the eye-roll was obvious even so. Cube and his partner had to be part of any targeting against Iona.

Morrison leveled his gaze around the table. "The rest of you be ready to move on a moment's notice based on any new information they discover. I have other agents standing by as well. We won't be caught off-guard. Any questions?"

Broadcast raised his first finger in a half-wave. "How certain are we of the info that was intercepted? Is it the real deal? We've been trying to break into their servers for a while now."

Morrison nodded in Teal's direction. "We have a new expert on board. They spent all night breaking in and copying all the Movement's files."

Teal tapped the table. "And I added a backdoor access point for us to use anytime we want. It's undetectable from either side. And I spoofed several screennames our agents can use to infiltrate their chatrooms."

Cast leaned on his elbows and looked down the table at them. "And you are?"

"Teal. I started last week. Working nights for now, so I'm about off shift."

Gator cleared her throat. "Teal is new, but has a wealth of possible skills to provide the bureau."

Cast looked like he didn't dare argue with Gator.

Two more questions, offers to help with the tech team really, and Morrison dismissed the meeting.

Sven grinned at Iona and Carlos. "Does that mean we're helping the techs or just hanging around until we're called?"

"I have some reports to review and email to check," Carlos said with a shrug. "So hanging around, I guess."

Iona pushed the coffee cup back to Sven. "I have to report to Doc Choi before I do anything else. Thanks for the coffee."

"You're welcome. Maybe we can meet up for lunch?"

They both answered with echoes of his 'maybe'. Everyone stood and wandered out of the room. Any thoughts Sven had of walking with Iona were thwarted when she headed off with her friend Lisa, deep in conversation.

He went through the break room and washed his coffee cup, refilled it, and wandered back to his cube. Might be some busy work there until he was needed someplace. Around lunchtime, Broadcast called him. *"Hey, Left, you busy?"*

"Naw. What do you need?"

"Lunch, mostly. I've got a delivery coming to the main entrance. Can you pick it up for me? It's under my name."

Asshole. But it was better than sitting here. *"Got it."*

The delivery person was waiting at the security desk when Sven exited the elevator. Almost too late, Sven dug out his wallet to find cash for a tip. The young woman held up her free hand. "Tip was already paid. Thanks, though. You Sven?" Her smile reached her eyes and those eyes were checking him out, from his lips to his chest to lower than his chest and back to his lips.

"That's me. I'll get this upstairs. Thanks." He returned the smile, but not the study of her body. She looked barely eighteen. As the elevator doors closed, he laughed at the restaurant name on the bag. The 'close but not good' place

Iona had turned down yesterday. He was still chuckling when he handed the bag to Cast.

"What?" Cast peered into the bag. "Is something wrong with it?"

Sven just grinned. "Just a joke I heard the other day. Enjoy your lunch." He strolled back to his cube, leaving Cast to wonder what was up. Even if it was the less good place, the smell had his hunger woken. *"Carlos? Ready to break for lunch?"*

"I have to work through lunch and relying on my emergency stash for food. Try for an early dinner?"

"Sure."

A lonely sandwich from the shop on the corner would be enough for now. In the elevator, his finger hesitated over the button for the infirmary level, but he jammed the street level button. He couldn't be sure Iona was done with Choi yet. Or that she was still down there. They could find her before dinner.

One turkey-cranberry sauce-cream cheese on whole wheat later, he was back in the elevator to his cubicle, wondering how he was going to fill the rest of the day.

"Johansen." Morrison filled the space as the elevator doors opened. "You done with that assignment yet?"

"Assignment?" he asked before his brain thought better of it.

"Read your damn email and get started."

Sven nodded and squeezed past Morrison. He'd checked email before getting lunch, right?

"You okay?" Carlos asked, concern coloring his thoughts.

"Yeah, just missed an email and got caught."

"Morrison?"

"Yep. Nearly back to my desk. Hope it something I can get to quickly."

He dropped into his chair and opened the email. Sent two hours ago. Yikes.

"If it's what I think it is, you'll be fine. Iona said she's free for dinner. Italian place on Oak? Five-thirty-ish?"

"Sounds good. Thanks."

He quick-read the email once, then again slowly. Ah. The login name and password for one of the accounts Teal created for them to access the Freedom Movement sites and instructions to get familiar with the site and the regular commenters there before engaging and infiltrating.

On-line undercover where no one sees your face and you sleep in your own bed at night. He logged in and started poking around.

"Knock knock."

Sven looked up, first at the time, then at Carlos in his cube's doorway. "How is it after five already?"

"Having fun, then?"

Sven gestured at his screen and the three different Movement pages open there. "I guess. Lots to look at anyway. They're really in favor of Full Disclosure and all the ways they can possibly force the government into it."

"Yeah." Carlos perched on the edge of the desk, leaving his head still taller than Sven's, but closer than when he was standing. It was odd, being the short one, but Carlos deserved to look down on him once in a while. "Find any new plots?"

"Don't think so. Mostly been in the forums where they're all trying to out-do each other with over-the-top suggestions. Rigging the soccer finals is a really popular one."

"Luckily for the league, the people in charge of the Movement seem to have realized that proving they tampered with the games would be hard."

"My personal favorite was the plan to have a metal controller push a racecar into a wall, then have another rogue amp stop the wreck at the last minute in full view of the crowd."

"That one was good. Did you see the one suggesting they get an electricity controller during winter storms to repair power outages before the utility crews did?"

"I missed that one."

"A couple of them shut it down pretty quickly. Not provable. Ready for dinner?"

"Uh-huh." Sven logged out of all the Movement sites, tabbed over to his email and sent an already-written report to Morrison. "Got everything?"

Carlos held up his jacket and backed up to give Sven room to stand and get his coat.

"Walking or driving?"

"Driving, and we're giving Iona a ride."

Sven stretched. That was more concentrated sitting than he'd realized. "Where's she meeting us?" Coat in hand, he followed Carlos along the aisle between cubicles.

"Somewhere along the way."

The floor was quiet – just past quitting time for the day shift staff. They had the elevator to themselves down to the parking garage where the door opened to frame Iona against the dingy yellow concrete wall.

She still wore the jeans and light blue fitted t-shirt from this morning, but now her hair was brushed loose from the ponytail and framed her face, glowing under the lame fluorescent lights of the parking garage. Sven shook his head. "Honestly, how does your hair manage to look better than anyone else's under these lights?"

"Just lucky, I guess." But she flipped her hair over one shoulder and smiled. She fell into step alongside them, beside Carlos, not Sven. "Just got word about Roth. Choi gets to work with him for two more days, then he's off to regional containment."

"You know your heart rate's up, right?" Carlos said.

"Shut up. So's yours." He pulled keys free from his pocket. "That's good. Two days longer than I'd like him here, but at least there's a plan." A beautiful woman who was a friend and colleague. Nothing wrong with appreciating her looks. Besides, she wasn't interested in him that way.

He unlocked all the doors with his key fob. Carlos waved Iona to the front seat and took the seat behind her.

Sven got in and started the engine. "Italian place is fine with you?" he asked Iona.

"Sure, I like that place." She settled back into the seat and fastened the seat belt. "Did both of you end up checking out Freedom Movement websites?"

Sven nodded. "All afternoon."

At the same time, Carlos added, "Yeah."

"Did you see where they hoped they'd get video of me next time?"

Sven tapped the brakes harder than intended at the garage's exit. "Shit. No, I didn't see that."

"I saw that one," Carlos said. "They didn't use your name, but it sounds like someone there knows who you are."

"Should we ask to keep you out of the limelight for a while?"

Iona shook her head. "I'll just be careful. They've gotten invites for me, Breeze, and Typhoon to the Foresters' conference next Friday. There won't be any reason for me to blast fire there."

Sven neatly parallel parked only half a block from the restaurant. They ordered at the counter – fettucine alfredo for Iona, chicken marsala for him, and ravioli with mushrooms for Carlos – and sat at a booth in the back. Sven sat across from Iona. Carlos hesitated before sliding in beside Sven.

They talked about the weather until their salads and bread were delivered. Talking about the food and whether olive oil or butter was better on the bread got them through until their plates arrived.

The music was the perfect volume, soft enough to allow conversation, but loud enough to mask voices from neighboring booths. Once they started eating, it felt safe to talk about work. Sven rested his fork against his plate. "When does the conference start?"

Iona set her glass down. "Monday, but the Vice President and Governor will only be there on Friday. That's when we're going to be there."

Carlos shrugged. "A week to plan all of this. Plenty of time. I'm worried about them knowing you, though."

Sven nodded and pulled his attention from her lips. She hadn't been into their fake kiss, why was it still on his mind? "I wish they'd let us bring in Cube."

Iona swallowed and shook her head. "Not him. It's Roth. And whoever he's talking to." She looked Sven in the eye. "Did he tell you what I asked about?"

"Last night?"

She wasn't interested in him, he could at least talk up the guy she liked. "Mostly, he talked about how amazing you are."

She twisted to face Carlos. "Wait, really?"

He shrugged again and looked from her to Sven and back. Sven kept his emotions wrapped up tight. She was definitely interested in Carlos. Anything Sven said aloud or telepathically might spook him.

Iona's mouth curved into a small smile. "Sorry. About whether something or someone could block whoever is talking to Roth. Is that something any of our mentals could do?"

Sven shook his head. "No, he didn't tell me about that."

She shrugged. Her shirt was tight enough that he could clearly see breasts move in harmony with her shoulders. He forced his attention to her face. She liked Carlos, he shouldn't be slavering over her like a starving dog.

"I just wondered if we had anyone on our side who could keep prisoners from unsupervised conversations with those outside. It would help in a lot of ways." She leaned back and sipped her water.

Sven wished he'd gotten wine with dinner. The selection here was limited, but decent and affordable. "I can see how it would. I really hope they haven't found anyone on their side who can block our communications."

Carlos waved a forkful of Ravioli. "That's what I said." He finished the bite from the fork. "It would keep him from telling his friends on the outside about us."

"I don't know if it's been tried. I'm pretty sure we can't put a block over a building. Maybe block one person from receiving or sending. We might have to know the exact location." Sven turned to Carlos. "What do you think? Want to try later? We can get Cast as our guinea pig."

"I'm in. I'm not sure it'll work. If we could, wouldn't someone have done it already? It seems like something we'd talk about."

"True. If it can keep our people safe, it's worth a try." Too late to keep them from finding out about Iona. But maybe they could protect other identities *and* keep the Movement from finding out any more about Iona.

Iona smiled. "And maybe it's something that takes the two of you together."

Carlos grinned back at her. "We are good at working together."

His grin was suspicious, but the mental image he supplied reminded Sven of the time they'd pranked Cast with a water balloon.

"Touché." Sven took another bite of the chicken marsala. Dinner was almost over, he realized with a surprising amount of regret. It's not like he's not going to be working with Iona all next week. "How are plans shaping up for the conference? Will you have much to do?"

Iona shook her head and finished her mouthful. Sven kept his attention away from her mouth.

"Mostly researching the Movement's activities between now and the conference. When we're there, we'll mostly be watching for trouble and ready to act on it. Unless they let more of their plans slip, we have to be ready for anything."

"Any chance of getting more bureau agents in as security?" Three of them in a crowd of civilians wasn't all that encouraging.

Carlos swirled the water in his glass. "A full detail of secret service and city police will be present. And we'll just be a few thoughts away."

"See, couldn't be safer." Iona grinned before draining her water. "I'm sure we'll arrange several agents outside the building. Who's the one from Seattle who can phase through walls? Maybe we can borrow her for the week. We have plenty of telepaths, telekinetics, and fighters locally."

"We can watch her from anywhere, right?" Sven asked Carlos.

"No problem. Only if she lets us, though."

"Duh. Flames burn."

Iona dabbed her lips with her napkin.

Flame is hot when she's not making fire. Sven kept his eyes from her mouth and sent Carlos a mental nudge to appreciate her.

"It's not like I don't see it. You're just wrong about where she's looking." Carlos placed his fork and knife across his plate. "Are we ready to take Iona back before she turns into a pumpkin?"

She stood in a single graceful motion. "Wrong fairy tale. I'm the fire-breathing dragon." She looked around the mostly empty restaurant. "But I do have a schedule to keep. We're not that far from the bureau. I can walk if you need to head the other direction."

They joined her on the way to the entrance. "No problem, we're going that way." Sven got ahead of her in time to open the door.

Iona froze in the doorway before ducking her head to one side and slipping between the two of them.

"Something wrong?" Sven said, leaning so close his lips brushed her hair.

"Not sure." Her voice was low. "Across the street. Is that the woman who was with Cube?"

He glanced over her head, as if looking at Carlos, but scanning the sidewalk opposite. Two women, one standing and one walking, matched Cube's partner in build and hair color. "Too far to be sure." He rested on hand on the small of her back and shielded her from the street as Carlos unlocked the car doors. *"Wonder twin powers activate. See if we can pick up anything."*

"I can't tell if they're watching us. No one seems to be thinking about us." Carlos answered. *"One did just put their phone away. Camera, maybe?"*

Iona took the back seat. Sven tried to nudge Carlos into joining her, but he refused. "Am I just imagining it?"

Carlos buckled his seat belt and turned his head to see over the seat. "I caught them too late to tell. We'll have the team scour the web for any pictures of you and scrub them away."

"All the bad guys know where we work. Following us from there isn't that hard." Iona slid low in the seat. "You two be careful going home. Make sure you're not followed."

When he pulled the car up to the front of the bureau offices, Iona leaned between them and pressed a kiss on his cheek, then Carlos's. Just a quick little 'thank you' kiss, but he felt it more than those 'fake date' kisses from the other day. Did she mean it more, or was he just overreacting? Hopefully Carlos felt the same, or more, from his kiss. If only Carlos would act on the mutual attraction that was so thick Sven couldn't see through it.

CHAPTER SEVEN

Iona hopped out of Sven's car and thanked them again for the ride to and from dinner. She kept her head down so they wouldn't see the blush burning across her face. Kissing them, really? How foolish was she? Not dating guys from the bureau was her long-standing rule. She didn't need the complications. Dating Sven or Carlos would mess up her working relations with both of them. At least pecks on their cheeks fell into the 'friendly thanks' category of kisses. As long as *they* interpreted them that way.

Her phone buzzed with the 'urgent message' tone when she'd taken three steps from the car she held up one hand to signal Sven to wait.

He understood and the car idled at the curb while she opened the message. *Shit.*

The guys must have the same message. Their faces went pale and they jumped from the now-parked car.

The message was short enough. 'Roth escaped. Three injured. Unknown rogues possibly still in building.'

Iona reached the entrance first and swiped her badge. Both guys were at her heels through the doors and into the elevator. "Did you get any more details?" she asked, jabbing the button for the infirmary floor.

Carlos nodded. "Only that he had help – at least two others broke in and broke him out."

"Is that who they think is still inside?"

Sven glanced at his phone. "No one saw them leave, so they don't know if any are still here or how many."

The elevator settled to a stop. Iona raised her brow at him. "Good thing we have some telepaths around."

Sven blew out a breath and looked at Carlos. "I hope we're enough."

They raced through the floor to the holding cells. Fire suppressant foam covered the floor surrounding the security station. Footprints tracked in all directions, overlapping and from at least three different sizes of shoes.

Carlos went behind the desk; the chair was toppled and marks in the foam showed where someone or something was dragged away. Carlos pointed at the video screens. "No one's showing up on any of these."

"Good." Iona moved to Carlos's side. "Are you picking up any sense of someone hiding here?"

Sven and Carlos shared a look – the kind that went with their telepathic communication. Iona watched the screens for movement or signs of life while they did their thing.

Sven finally spoke. It seemed like they took forever, but the clock in the corner of the video screens said it had barely been three minutes. "No one here now. We thought we sensed something, but only for a fraction of a second then it was gone. There's a few people up on the 2nd floor already. We're supposed to join them when we can."

Something moved on one of the video screens. "Do we have time to check Roth's cell? I think there's something there."

"They said 'when we can'," Sven repeated. "But we're all going. I'll tell them we're here."

Sven insisted on leading the way. No issues with that, Iona followed, looking for signs of fire along the fire-resistant concrete walls. A couple of streaks where the grey was shinier might be the result of a blast of fire. Inconclusive at best. The door to Roth's cell was ajar. Sven looked back past Iona and nodded at Carlos. A few seconds of silence between them and Sven pulled the door fully open.

Iona passed Sven with a hand on his shoulder. Traces of the fire suppressant foam from yesterday streaked the floor. The cot, wall-mounted desk, and toilet corner were all intact. A single sheet of paper, charred around the edges fluttered on the side of the cot.

"Oh." She took the paper by one corner. "This is all."

"It's something, though." Carlos read the words written in bold black ink. "'We know who you are and soon we'll tell the world'."

"Idle threats." Iona shook the paper gently. "They've been trying to tell the world about us for a while now."

Sven touched her elbow. "They have names and faces now. Better take that paper to the conference room. And we need to review the video. No one mentioned seeing it before."

She took another sweeping glance around the cell and nodded.

"Don't speak aloud, but did you see that?" Carlos's voice sounded in Iona's mind. *"A person-shaped mist?"*

She concentrated her thoughts at both men. *"There, in the corner."* If it was the same amp she'd heard of before, it was dangerous. *"Hold your breath and don't let it touch you."* She looked around the room again. "Yeah, nothing else here." She concentrated on the men again. *"You can hear me, right?"*

Both answered affirmative. Their mental voices different and familiar at the same time.

"Don't get between me and it. If it attacks, I'll see if it's flammable."

"Be careful," Carlos said as he stepped towards the open cell door.

Good idea. He should make sure the mist-person, if that's who it was, didn't close the door and lock them in.

Sven followed Carlos, keeping his face turned towards Iona. "Yeah, hope we can call it a night, now."

The mist thickened, but stayed in the corner. If it didn't attack, she couldn't justify flaming it, especially if she suspected it was really a person. There really wasn't any other obvious way to subdue to capture it. Them. The mist-person, if that's what it was.

Iona followed the guys to the door, then took one more look around. The mist tapered at the end at the ceiling and flowed towards the vent there. It stopped halfway through and sent a tendril towards the three of them. Not aggressive; probing or questioning.

Iona nudged Carlos with her shoulder. "Have I shown you I can do this?" She held both palms up and called up a ball of fire on each. With a bit of concentration, she flared the left one into a tear-drop, the top reaching higher than her head. After two seconds, she dropped that flame back to a ball and made the other a tear-drop. Three times through she switched sizes back and forth. "I'm working on juggling them, but this is how I fake it for now."

The mist tendril reversed and disappeared up the vent.

Once in the hallway, she closed and locked the door and watched through the window. The mist didn't return.

"Let's go." She led the way in a power walk. "Can you contact someone about the building design? I want to know where that vent leads. And ask someone to keep eyes on the monitors for all the cells."

"On it," Carlos said on her right.

Sven chuckled from her left. "Good show of strength back there. I think it means the mist-person is flammable."

"I hope someone has more info on them." Iona checked out the security desk as they passed it. "Whether they're always mist, or if they can take solid form. Lisa ran into them before and the mist was able to knock her out so they could capture her."

Sven nodded. "Then, thanks for telling us to hold our breath."

"I'm glad you could hear my thoughts. Only when you're linked?"

"Pretty much. It helps if we're close together, but knowing where each other are is good enough."

At the words 'close together', a warm feeling flowed down Iona's back. Warm and comforting. And just a little bit arousing. So, her body decided now that he was her type? Nope. No way was she getting between these two.

They reached the elevator and waited for it to show up.

"Got it," Carlos said. "Each cell has a vent that goes directly outside. Concrete block framing with three by five inch openings. The mist could flow in and out, but a solid person wouldn't fit."

"Should I stay there in case they return?" Iona half-turned.

"They're watching all the cells and a team's on the way to seal the doors so it won't get into the building if it goes back in a cell. If we've got someone able, we could seal off the outside of the vent and keep the mist inside if it returns."

She relaxed. "Good to know." Now Carlos's voice was making the warm tinglies. She checked the time. Not overdue yet, so that wasn't it. Could they be working together? Or using their empathy on her?

In the elevator, the men flanked her, putting her between them. Sven sighed. "If we're going to be called late this often, we should ask for sleeping quarters in the building."

"My bed won't fit three, but maybe we can ask for a couple of cots." *Shit, why did I say that? Oh shit, oh shit, oh shit, can they tell what I'm feeling?* What's up with her body now? No reaction to anyone for months, and now two guys. Two best friend guys? "I mean, there's plenty of open rooms downstairs. We can ask if some can be available for agents working on call."

The elevator opened before either man responded. *Saved by the bell.* Iona hurried out and headed for the conference room. Enough people there should keep her from saying anything else stupid.

'Enough people' for sure. The room was full, task force members from leaders on down, plus the heads of the security department. Iona slipped into an empty seat beside Lisa. Carlos took the last seat, across from Iona, leaving Sven to feel along the wall before leaning against it. Iona wished she'd thought to check the chair for a camo or invisible amp before sitting. She would have noticed the weight in the chair when she pulled it out, though.

Morrison rapped on the table for attention. "Finally. Report on what you three saw down there."

He was looking at her, so Iona spoke for them. "This note was in Roth's cell." She slid it down the table. "After we found it, we saw a person-shaped mist in the cell, then it left through a wall vent. We called for building services to seal all the doors in that hall in case it returns. If it's caught on video, I'd like Lisa and Lucent to see if it's the same one that knocked them out before."

"Good call." Morrison read the note as it was handed up to him. "No surprise here. Teal, tonight monitor all their internet activity for any mention of agent names and scrub them if they show up." He clicked a controller and stood aside as a projection filled the wall behind him.

Roth, sitting on the cot in his cell, as viewed from the ceiling camera. He had a magazine on his lap, but didn't look as though he was reading it. He glanced up at the wall opposite the door several times a minute.

All his glances were rewarded when a thick shadow-colored mist flowed in through the vent high on the wall. It coalesced into a person-shape in front of him for nearly a minute before flattening and oozing out under the door. Roth leaned back on his hands, a smug smile on his face.

Lisa sucked in air between her teeth. "That's either the same rogue who caught me outside Lucent's, or one with the same power. We never figured out what gas was used to knock us out."

Broadcast clucked his tongue. "Going to be a hard one to catch. Even harder to contain if we do."

"They backed away from fire, so we know that hurts them," Iona said. "But I'm always a last option for capture."

Morrison clicked his remote again. "But at least we have you if it comes down to that." The view changed to the corridor outside the cells, as viewed from the security station end. If they weren't looking for the mist, they wouldn't see it. The sheet of mist flowed up the corridor, staying along the side, pressed up against the wall. The mist paused before reaching security and formed an upright column, purple under the fluorescent lights.

The view shifted again to the ceiling above the security desk. The shadowy column floated up behind the guard typing up a report at the desk. Even suspecting what was going to happen, Iona gasped with the rest when the shadow reached out arms around the guard's face and held them there until he slumped unconscious. The shadow arms released his face and reached for his belt and unclipped the badge there and carried it back up the corridor.

Another view change, back to the cell. The badge slid under the door, followed by a sheet of shadow-mist. Roth lifted it with two fingers and held it out as the smoke coalesced back into a human shape. They appeared to be talking, but sound wasn't recorded. The mist-person took the badge back from Roth and flowed back out the vent.

"The next video is several minutes later. We have records from the entrance scanner showing the guard's badge used to enter." Morrison started the next video.

The guard was still slumped over his desk, visibly breathing thank goodness, but still. An unknown person with a blue jacket and light hair—Iona couldn't tell if it was grey or blond in the video—approached the desk, looked around, unclipped the keys from the guard's belt, and disappeared up the hall.

Morrison clicked and the display split to the corridor and cell. Inside the cell, the smoke person and Roth stood at the door. Outside the door, blue jacket used the guard's key and badge for two of the three locks then stood back. The keypad remained untouched but the man turned the handle and pulled the door open.

Questions sounded around the table. Broadside asked, "Is he a mental? Kinetically pressing the keys after grabbing the code from the guard's mind?"

Teal shook their head. "Telekinesis and telepathy together in one person are pretty rare. I'm guessing it's either telekinesis or metal control to move the tumblers in the lock."

Morrison tapped the table. "The rogue is unknown, name and power."

Teal raised a hand, "Can I suggest we just call them 'Mist' until we have an actual name for them?"

Morrison shrugged. "Fine by me. Without more evidence, all we can be sure of here is that it was able to unlock the door." He gestured to the video where the three, Roth, Mist, and the new one, had reached the guard's station. Another bureau guard approached the station from the other side. Mist flowed over and surrounded the guard's head until she drooped to the floor.

The three headed to the staircase instead of the elevator and the video rejoined them in the parking garage. Mist went first, flowing out to a shadow along the ceiling, Roth and the other strolled confidently to a car parked nose out in a spot just five along from the stairway.

Blue jacket unlocked the car and Mist hovered beside the driver's window after blue jacket slid behind the wheel. Roth whirled and looked back. Back in the direction of the elevator, Iona realized. He fired two blasts of flame and leaped into the passenger seat as the car sped away with a squeal of tires against the concrete.

Morrison clicked off the video. "Two agents were after them, one is in the infirmary with burns on their arms."

"His power is unknown," a deep voice said from the wall opposite the entrance. Lucent? "The surveillance team sees him at the headquarters and on break-ins. They call him 'Mac' or 'Mackenzie'. We don't know whether it's a first name, last name, or a nickname."

Morrison nodded. "Good. Who's on surveillance tonight? Bark?"

"Yessir."

"And he knows to watch for them?

Broadcast waved his hand at face level. "I told him. No word yet on whether they've shown up at their h.q."

Morrison hmm'ed. "Stay on duty tonight, Broadcast. You're our contact."

Broadcast's mouth dropped open then snapped shut. Iona glanced around to see how Carlos and Sven reacted. It was hard to be sure, she didn't know them that well yet, but Sven seemed smugly pleased and Carlos relieved at their release from night duty.

"All right then. Assignments for tonight." Morrison powered up his laptop and projected the screen on the wall. He typed as he spoke. "Broadcast, you're on constant contact with Bark. Lassie, I know it's harder to track a car than a person, but see if you can tell which direction Roth went from here in case they don't return to their base. Lucent, back her up so she can focus.

"Left and Right, you're still on-call. Listen for any agents needing assistance or backup. Teal, monitor the Movement's internet sites and shut down anything harmful. Flame, you're in the building anyway, help Teal out as necessary. Byte, go home and get some rest. You'll take over for Teal at oh-seven hundred sharp.

"As of this minute, there are no changes to the plans for the weekend. Flame, Typhoon, and Breeze will be inside the conference on the day the Vice President and Governor are there. Left, Right, and Broadcast will be as near as possible outside the building, along with bureau agents not on this task force. Any questions? No? Good. Meeting adjourned."

Lisa scurried out first, with a whoosh of air following that must be Lucent.

Carlos smiled across at Iona. "Thanks for going to dinner with us. We're going to be on-call from home, but we'll keep a listen if you need anything."

"Thanks. Living here means I can't ever count on a weekend off." Her smile back was met with a flash of those dimples. "Good luck getting out before they find an on-site task for you."

He looked from one end of the table to the other. Morrison was deep in conversation with Gator and Teal. Sven stood behind Carlos's chair. Carlos met Iona's eyes. "Good point. We're out."

Sven saluted her with a wink and followed Carlos out.

Iona waited until Teal was ready and caught up as they left the conference room. "My time is at your command, rookie."

Teal giggled. "I like the sound of that. This way, assistant." On the way, Teal chatted about Roth's escape and how they experienced it from inside the building. Luckily, two floors up from all the excitement. They each took a seat at a bank of monitors. "I guess you just need to open up as many screens as you can with Movement websites and sites they post on. Leave one screen for searching terms that will lead to posts about us. See if they've gone through with any disclosure, or mentioning any of us by name. Besides you and Dr. Choi, what other names would Roth know?"

"Probably some of the security team. They don't usually reveal their power so that should keep them safe. It's not like it's a secret who works here. Lisa and Lucent were part of the team that brought him in. I can ask her who else was on that team."

"Okay, open up some search windows and call her. I'll open more windows from this station."

Iona tapped in commands to open four windows on the multi-screen workstation, then dialed Lisa's number. "Straight to voice mail. She must be still tracking the car."

"Right. Try again later. We have enough search names for now." Teal pulled the keyboard onto their lap and kicked their Doc Martens-clad feet up onto the desk.

"Hey Iona," Sven said in Iona's mind. *"Lisa said you tried to call. She's busy now and asked me to check in."*

It was Sven's voice, but she sensed Carlos's presence as well.

She concentrated on thinking her reply. *"I was going to ask her which agents were there when Roth was taken into custody. Since they're threatening to reveal names, I'm searching the internet for names of agents that Roth might know."*

"Just a moment. I'll ask."

Iona scanned the windows open already. The 'official' Freedom Movement page didn't have any news or announcements of a sensitive nature. She opened the chat forum for the site. Lots of discussion of yesterday's events, applying credit and blame randomly, and rarely correctly.

"Iona?" Sven again, with Carlos in the background. *"Lisa named three who helped with capturing Roth, but she doesn't think he would have seen their powers or heard their names. You're the one most likely at risk."*

"Thanks. And thank her for me. Searching myself isn't egotistical at all is it?"

She felt more than heard Carlos laughing. Good to know her joke had landed. On another window, she ran a search for her name and her field name. Stupid to think 'Flame' wasn't going to have a bajillion hits. She tried again with 'Bureau Agent Flame' and 'Amp Flame'. The hits for 'Iona Sinclair', once she found ones that meant her, were pretty generic. The most recent was a mention of her getting a commendation for her fire-fighting at the upcoming forestry conference. A couple for some social media sites she used once in a while. Nothing accusing her of powers above and beyond the officially revealed strength and speed.

When she glanced over at Teal, she met Teal's gaze clearly watching her.

"What?"

"You were talking to your telepaths."

Iona felt heat in her cheeks. "They're not *my* telepaths. But, yeah, they passed on Lisa's answer."

"Which one do you like better?"

"They're both great to work with."

"No, I mean *like* like."

"What are we, in middle school?"

"I was trying to be PG. It's obvious when you look at them that you like them. Would you rather I asked which one's bones you want to jump?"

Iona kept her eyes on her monitors. "I have a personal rule to not date co-workers."

"Uh-huh."

"I do. It just messes things up."

"You should check your face in a mirror when you're around them. It says something else. And you should figure out which one of them you like more or it's going to get really confusing."

She buried herself in searching internet sites, only glancing Teal's way to make sure they weren't scanning the same sites. Finally, after a series of yawns, she stretched and checked the time. "It's nearly midnight and

I haven't found anything that points at us or about their plans for the conference. Is it okay if I call it a night?"

"Huh?" Teal looked over from their computer. "Sure. I can handle it from here. Get some sleep before they work you all day tomorrow. Maybe dream about your boys."

Teal's phrasing haunted Iona as she headed back to her room. Extra security personnel were in place at each elevator landing and at both the medical wing and the cell block wing of her floor. 'My boys'? She had no claim on either of them. And she shouldn't want to.

She closed the door to her room and leaned against it. Was Teal right? And what if they were? And worse, could Sven and Carlos tell? Past midnight by now, she washed her face and dropped onto her bed. She'd gone well over eighteen hours by now. Palm out, she called up a flame and held it steady. The tip wavered but she still tested it by sending the fire up each finger and back to her palm.

The fire faltered at the end, not returning to her palm from her pinkie. When she nudged it, it flared up and died. At least she hadn't needed precision tonight for anything. And it hadn't burned up anything here. Sigh. Eighteen hours was her interval for a reason.

She got a vibrator from the bedside drawer and stretched out on her bed.

"Iona?" Carlos said. *"Am I interrupting anything?"*

She tucked the vibrator under the duvet and focused on her reply. *"No, just getting ready for bed. Are you still working?"*

"I think we're done. Need to listen while we sleep for any calls, but it's been quiet. I wanted let you know Lisa got back safely. She tracked the car far enough to be sure it was headed for Movement headquarters. Bark spotted them arrive and got trackers on all the cars. Roth left there right after arriving, the car's being tracked."

"Thanks. You didn't have to let me know, but I appreciate it."

"I just didn't want you to worry. Goodnight."

"Goodnight." Iona could just sense a bit of Sven supporting Carlos, but only Carlos spoke. Their presence left her mind. Leaving her alone, in her bed, with her vibrator. Had either of them guessed? Sven might have after yesterday. Those anonymous hands were going to have to work hard to keep thoughts of Carlos's sweet smile and Sven's sparkling eyes out of mind. Not to mention their broad shoulders, trim waists, and nice legs.

Her dating rule was on the verge of collapse and she had no idea what to do about it.

CHAPTER EIGHT

Carlos slumped into the car Wednesday morning. "Sorry for running late." He handed Sven a travel mug of coffee. "I slept like crap. Worried about Iona on Friday."

"She'll be fine. Typhoon, Breeze, and a ton of secret service will be inside and we'll be outside. It's not today. Save your sleepless night for tomorrow."

"I know. I just wish I could keep her safe. I know it's stupid, she's better equipped to handle trouble than I am, but I can't help it."

"You like her."

"So do you."

Sven sighed and stopped at a light. He looked over. "And there's nothing we can do about it unless she says she likes one of us."

Carlos sipped from his coffee and stared into the lid. "We'll be okay if she does like one of us, right?"

Sven patted his shoulder. "It's always you and me, no matter what else happens or who else is around. She likes you better anyway."

Carlos shook his head. "Watch her feelings better next time we're talking to her. It's you she likes."

As soon as they hit their cubes, they got assignments – Sven staying at the office for communications and Carlos to check out the convention center and surroundings. By lunchtime, he'd finished the initial tour and was impressed with the security. Streamlined but controlled entrances and exits. There wasn't anything to stop Mist from slithering through a vent or under a door, but solid, visible people could be monitored. Hopefully, someone was working out a way to deal with Mist.

He checked in with Sven. *"I'm meeting with the event planner now, any questions for them? I'll get details on the setup for the conference."*

"Good timing. They want to know about the fire and smoke detectors in the building. If the smoke detectors track particles, they might spot Mist too."

He smiled at the convention center director and sat in her wood-paneled office. *"They didn't track them entering the cell."* The director pulled a sheet of paper from a cabinet, spread it across her desk, then adjusted the cuffs of her navy blazer.

"Apparently the cells have flame detectors, not smoke."

"Makes sense, if we have fire starters in them. Is Iona in the meetings with you?"

"Haven't seen her. I think she's in briefings with Breeze and Typhoon."

Carlos waited until the event director finished showing him the layout of the room for Friday's presentation to ask about fire detectors.

She started, then pushed aside the layouts and swung a computer monitor over. "Your bureau is about all kinds of safety, isn't it?"

"Exactly. Can I see the location and types of all the fire or smoke detectors?"

She fiddled with the mouse and keyboard. "There." On the display, tiny red circles lit up at semi-regular intervals. "These are the smoke detectors. They'll alarm at the point and in the central command center when they are exposed to a minimum level of particulate in the air." She tapped in more commands and orange circles lit up, mostly in the loading dock and over the cafes. "These alarm when open flames are present."

"Thank you. Are these files you can send us?"

She pursed her lips and looked up towards the ceiling. "I think I can. Let me get approval first. I'll send them later this afternoon if it's okay."

"Sure." He forwarded the information on to Sven for him to report out.

The director leaned back in her faux leather chair. "We have secret service and state police on site for Friday. They'll be directing our in-house security team. Neither have mentioned your involvement at all. Will there be any problems over jurisdiction?"

"Some of our people are being honored for their efforts in last season's forest fires. We'll have a few stationed outside for support, but they'll be discrete."

She looked him over, tapped one finger against the desktop. "Right. See that there's nothing that disrupts my facility."

"Preventing public disruptions is what the bureau's all about. Thank you for the tour and the information." Carlos stood and offered his hand.

Her handshake was the same as the one she greeted him with, firm and authoritative. "I'll email those files as soon as I have permission."

On his way out to the bureau car – in non-descript white with official plates that made it difficult to hide – Carlos checked in. *"Who am I reporting to with this info?"*

"Gator's leading the briefing with Iona and the others. Probably her?"

"Okay, on my way back now."

Interesting. He'd never talked directly to Gator. She took her leadership role seriously and since she lived in the gated community with the other pheno amps to hide from the normals, she didn't interact with other agents after work.

Back in the parking garage, he checked the car in with the transportation desk and sent a text to Morrison reporting his return and asking where to go next. He was still on the stairs when his phone pinged with Morrison's reply directing him to a conference room.

He stopped only long enough to use the washroom and slipped into the room, keeping the door as quiet as possible. Every face turned toward him anyway.

Gator sat at the head of the table – the lapels of a grey linin suit jacket calling attention to her beautifully sculpted leathery green face. Carlos nodded quickly at her eye contact, then ducked his head and took a seat. He placed his phone on the table and studied the image of a map projected on the wall.

Gator said, "Now that Mr. Martinez is here, we can fill in the building part of the map." She waved a laser pointer at the squarish box outlined near the center of the map. "Before we do, are there any questions about the route the VIPs will take to the convention center and our parts along it?"

Carlos scanned the table. Heads of a few different departments were there, along with Iona, Breeze, Typhoon, some of the tech crew, and some general security types. One woman raised a hand. Carlos recognized her from the security team.

"Before my people ask, overtime is already approved for this, right?"

Gator nodded. "The budget isn't open-ended, but stopping whatever the Movement has planned is high-priority and overtime for everything associated has been approved."

Carlos's phone lit up and a message received icon appeared. He pulled it close. The director had sent the requested files. Probably what Gator was waiting for.

"If there are no more questions, Mr. Martinez, can you report on the status of the interior of the convention center?"

He held out his phone. "They just sent the layout schematics. May I connect?" At her nod, he plugged his phone into the projection system and opened the file. Clearing his throat, he described the building's layout, the planned seating arrangement for Friday night's presentations, the likely stationing of security, and locations of both kinds of fire detectors. He kept his eyes on the screen as he pointed out everything until his final, "Any questions?"

Breeze raised a hand. "Can you show the chair arrangement one for the main hall again? We were planning on the three of us spreading out instead of sitting together, right? Should we choose our area now?"

Gator waved a hand at the image. "Sounds good. Go ahead."

Breeze took the left side of the room, Typhoon the right, and Iona the back. Carlos dropped color-coded spots for each of them onto the image.

Gator faced the projection, one hand on her hip. "We're there first to protect the VIPs, then the civilians, then to protect amp confidentiality. Ms. Sinclair will better serve closer to the front." Gator turned to Iona. "Make sure you're within range of the stage, someplace where those around you won't be in the line of your fire if you need to use it."

"If I have to use fire in that space, our confidentiality is up in smoke." A couple of people giggled at Iona's pun, but Carlos couldn't tell whether it was intentional.

Gator held up one finger. "Number one, protect the Governor and Vice President, number two protect civilians, confidentiality is third. Clear?"

Iona nodded. "Got it."

"Besides," Gator added. "We've got staff who are very good at reframing memories if it's necessary."

There was a distinct note of bitterness there. Not that Carlos could blame her. Full disclosure would benefit the pheno amps more than anyone else. Letting the Freedom Movement make the disclosure would crater any public trust in the bureau or for amps in general. How the government was going to manage it smoothly was anyone's guess. *And the longer they take, the worse it's bound to be.*

By the awkward shared looks around the table, Carlos didn't pick up on her bitterness just through empathetic reading. Vocal and physical cues work.

Iona reached across the table for Carlos's phone and tapped the image. A new dot appeared on the wall image near the front of the seating. "If I sit around here, I can reach any troublemakers on stage, or approaching the stage. Anything I fire would go over the heads of anyone in the rows in front of me."

"Better," agreed Gator. "We haven't been able to get reserved seating, so you'll have to plan ahead. I'll see if the security staff can help us out there, but don't count on it. Now, Mr. Martinez, what about security cameras? Can we tap into any in that meeting hall?"

He scaled back the map view to show the adjacent spaces and tapped several black dots on the map. "The cameras are mostly watching entrances and exits. These two will see everyone enter and exit the room, but there aren't any focused on the center of the room or the stage." He drew a large oval in the rear center of the room. "News cameras and reporters will be stationed here. One from each of the major networks, two local stations, and a few others. None of them are planning on a live broadcast, but we should be able to hack into their feeds as they're recording."

"Good." Gator stood and placed both palms on the table. "Before you go tonight, I want telepaths to pair up with their firefighter and work out how communication will go on Friday. Yes, Mr. Johansen, I know your group is three."

Carlos disconnected his phone from the room's projector and slipped it into his pocket. Sven and Iona rounded the table to join him.

"Our cubes or hers?" Sven asked.

Iona shook her head; her hair was up in a ponytail today and the end swung with the movement. "Let's get one of the little meeting rooms."

The first two of the little rooms were taken, but the third was open. Iona took the seat facing the door and Carlos sat across. Sven had to scrounge a chair from somewhere else and roll it in.

Once the door was closed, Iona started, "Is this going to be any different from me just talking to you in my head?"

"That might be all it is," Sven said. "But, if you want, we can access your eyes and ears to watch what's going on."

She pursed her lips. "How invasive is it?"

"Not very." Sven answered as Carlos said, "It's not like we'll see any more thoughts than we do when you're thinking them at us directly."

"Right," Sven continued. "It's like a short-cut. You just won't have to describe everything going on for us."

"Oookay. Close your eyes." Iona pulled out a pad of paper. *"Are you listening now?"*

The voice in his mind was hesitant but warm, only slightly nervous. *"I can hear you."* Carlos focused on the words from her mind with his eyes tightly closed.

"Me too." Sven's voice was the one he used when he was trying to project confidence, but Carlos sensed an underlying hopefulness.

"Go ahead and try to see through my eyes now." Iona thought.

Carlos expanded his senses through the mental connection, focusing on the visual cortex. With his eyes closed, he clearly saw himself and Sven. Sven had the little wrinkles between his eyes that he got when he concentrated really hard. Carlos smoothed out some hairs sticking out above his ear and Sven snickered.

"Can you read this?" She took a pen and wrote on the paper.

"National Association of Forestry Management Annual—" Sven broke off. *"What's that word? Conversation?"*

Carlos studied her handwriting, a mix of print and cursive. *"Convention."* His smile looked weird, backwards from his image in a mirror.

A twist of embarrassment from Sven and Iona. Carlos looked through Iona's eyes at the paper again. "Her handwriting isn't that bad."

"Gee, thanks. At least tomorrow, you won't have to depend on reading it."

The view through her eyes shifted as her chair squeaked. *"If this is enough testing, you can open your eyes."*

Sven leaned his elbows on the table. "How's your head? Tired, achy?"

Iona's ponytail brushed her cheek as she rolled her neck from side to side. "Doesn't seem bad. I could tell you were there, but it's about the same as talking to you. The speeches and stuff shouldn't last more than a couple of hours. If it gives me a headache, I'll take some aspirin when we finish."

Sven's eyes softened and Carlos could feel sympathy coming off him in waves. "We can always back off, too."

"I promise to let you know if it's too much for me." Iona checked the time. "Think they'll let us sign out now?"

Carlos checked his phone. "They'd better. We'll be out late tomorrow. And we were here late last night."

Sven opened the door. *"I'll grab my keys. You need anything from your desk?"*

"Nah." Carlos let Iona go out first.

"Meet you at the elevator." Sven headed off with a wave.

Another ploy of Sven's to let Carlos talk to Iona alone? Why doesn't he see that she's obviously more interested in him?

He stood beside her, neither pressing the elevator call button while they waited for Sven. "We haven't decided on dinner yet; do you want to join us?"

Iona shook her head. "I need to mentally prep for the mission, but thanks." She peered at him closely. "You okay? You seem a bit off today. I'm here to listen if you need to talk."

Carlos sighed and studied his hands. "That could be awkward."

"Only if you want to."

It's the only way we'll know. He took a deep breath and blew it out slowly. "You know how Sven and I can feel people's emotions, even when we're not trying to, right?"

She nodded.

"I've gotten the impression that you like Sven and he thinks you like me. And both of us like you. We don't know what to do without knowing how you feel about it... About us, I mean." Another deep breath and he shyly met her eyes. "Like I said, awkward. And you don't have to say."

Iona gave a nervous chuckle. "The problem is, you're both right and I don't know what to do about it." She grasped his hand and gave it a squeeze. An elevator arrived to let Teal out onto the floor and Iona slipped inside. "See you tomorrow."

Today Teal wore Doc Martens with a fluffy skirt, high-necked leotard, and a fedora. "Are you guys staying to help me search forums with bad grammar again?"

"It's all yours tonight." As they walked away, Carlos pondered his own polo shirt and jeans and wondered if Teal's flare for fashion might rub off on him with enough exposure.

"Coming. Call elevator."

Sven strode up just as the door opened. "Perfect timing. Thanks for waiting."

"You drove." Carlos let Sven monologue about choices for dinner – take-out, eating out, cooking together, or just eating on their own for a change.

Halfway to his car, Sven slowed his walk. "You're not listening are you?"

"Sure I am. Eating at home would be nice, my place, your place, or separate. Whatever you want."

They slid into the seats and Sven twisted to face him. "What did she say?"

There never were any secrets between them. There couldn't be.

"She likes both of us and doesn't know what to do about it."

"Oh."

"Yeah. Tomorrow won't be awkward at all."

CHAPTER NINE

Sven woke with an uncomfortable hard-on. His last dream was only vague images and scents, but it left him aroused. He was sure that Iona was part of it, and so was Carlos. He was used to Carlos being in his head, but not so much in his dreams. Especially not that kind of dream.

His shower was going to have to be a little bit longer this morning. Good thing they weren't expected in until later. Instead of a cold shower, he left it nice and warm and took care of the erection the manual way. After, he relaxed and leaned against the wall and let the warm water run over his shoulders.

"Want me to drive today?"

He turned off the water and grabbed a towel. *"Sure. Did you have weird dreams about us?"*

"Like, us us?"

"Uh-huh. And Iona."

"Maybe. None of the details are sticking, but there was definitely weirdness. Probably what we get for talking about her on the way home last night. Ready to go in forty-five?"

"Sure." Sven lifted a foot to the counter and dried it off. Carlos managed to surprise him yet again. His shy choir-boy self didn't sound at all embarrassed by those dreams. And it sounded like they were the same kind of dreams. Other foot dried, he toweled his hair and shaved.

Waiting in a van outside the convention center required comfy yet moderately professional clothes. A navy polo and his best khaki slacks fit the bill. He wondered what Iona would wear to the conference. *Not my business.* Besides, she looked good in anything.

Plenty of time for a real breakfast. Cinnamon-apple oatmeal, grapefruit, and coffee. He still ate quickly and puttered around after rinsing his dishes. Thinking about spending the day linked with Carlos and Iona after last night's dream wasn't exactly relaxing.

Three quick raps on his door signaled that Carlos was ready to go. Sven dropped his phone into one pocket, made sure his badge was clipped to the other, and opened the door. "Whoa, look at you all snazzy. Is that a new shirt?"

Carlos put his hands on his hips and posed like a model. The navy blue button-down shirt had silver threads in helix-like stripes. "With Teal in the office, I figured I should step up my game. Mom gave it to me a couple years ago." He pointed at his feet. "The boots, too." Tips of sliver-embroidered cowboy boots extended from his navy slacks.

"Now I feel underdressed." Sven locked his door and followed his partner down the steps. "But the boots give you at least another inch."

Carlos froze at the lobby door. "Is that why you think I'm wearing them?"

"Sorry, I didn't mean it like that. You're wearing them because they're cool and from your mom. They're perfect with the shirt, too."

Carlos blew out a breath. "I didn't even think about the heel. You don't think Iona will think I'm trying to be closer to her height, do you?"

"She won't notice over how awesome that shirt is." Did that mean Carlos was hoping? Sven caught his breath. What was he hoping for? Iona and Carlos as a couple would be great. A tiny part of him hoped he and Iona could give it a try, but he would honestly be happy for them. It would be less messy all around if she didn't settle for either of them, but Carlos deserved the happiness.

"It is pretty great. I might wear more of the ones Mom keeps sending me for a change." They made it all the way to the car and inside before Carlos added, "Do you think we'll manage it today? All three of us?"

"We're professionals. And it's all about keeping everyone inside safe."

Once at work, they checked for assignments and times. There was enough time for Sven to read all his emails and drink a fresh cup of coffee.

Carlos spoke in his mind, "*They have a van ready for us at one. Us, Cast, and Livewire in the van with a bunch of techies. We're to blend in with all the other news vans. Iona, Breeze, and Typhoon will take their own cars. Or carpool."*

Sven leaned back in his chair and closed the windows on his computer. *"And they probably didn't pack snacks yet. I'll go organize something."*

By the time he had enough food and drinks packed, they were assembled in a meeting room and bustled down to a huge van kitted out inside with workstations, monitors, and seats for all. Cast had the driver seat, Livewire in the other front seat. Teal and Byte were the 'bunch of techies'. Three workstations were mounted along each side of the back of the van – techs in the first seats behind the drivers. Sven and Carlos took the next two stations.

Sven nudged Teal. "Didn't you work last night?"

They smiled and shrugged. "Not all night. I'm the new broadcast siphoning engineer."

"Glad you're aboard then. Pass the word that I brought snacks."

"We can all hear you," Byte said from beside Teal. "If there's a coke, hand it over."

Broadcast swung into the driver's seat. "Everyone ready? The firefighters already set out."

Byte dropped the hand reaching for the soda Sven was handing her. "Whoa, you're driving?" She shook her head. "Got any stronger drinks in there?"

Cast started the van. "Har. Har. Buckle up everyone. Next stop, the parking lot of the convention center."

"Hey, want to check in with Iona?" Carlos asked.

"Uh – Okay. Get the awkwardness out of the way I guess."

Carlos did the talking. *"Just testing the communications. We're in the van and on our way. Are you almost there?"*

"Testing? Did you think it wouldn't work?" Iona's voice was teasing, no hint of awkwardness. *"We just got here and we're heading in to get our conference badges."*

Sven let Carlos answer. *"Cool. Want us to start watching now? Or wait until you're seated inside?"*

Just a little bit of unease from Iona, but Carlos felt Sven's stomach butterflies. *"Go ahead,"* she replied. *"Better to have some extra eyes on the scene."*

"They're ready to go inside," Sven told the rest of the van. "We'll be in contact with Flame from here on out."

Livewire looked back, her rainbow-dyed hair swinging across her eyes as she turned her head. "Got it. I'm with Typhoon."

Cast raced onto the freeway, merging with traffic. "I'm gonna wait until we're closer. Someone send a message along to Breeze."

Iona followed Breeze and Typhoon into the main entrance. A registration table full of smiling volunteers greeted them. Iona headed for the end labeled with 'R-Z' and presented her bureau identification to receive a conference badge and a program.

"What's the range on your telekinesis?" she asked, standing out of the way and looking at the program.

Sven made eye contact with Carlos who nodded. "Testing."

Through Iona's eyes, they focused on the cover of her conference program. A lift and a nudge and the top right corner fluttered at her in a little wave.

"Good enough?" Carlos asked. *"We'll be closer soon. What's your plan until the speeches start?"* As usual, Carlos had his eyes closed while watching through someone else's. Sven always watched it as a sort of overlay against his own view of the real world.

Iona looked over the reception area. Breeze was still in line for her badge and Typhoon was getting coffee at a stand. *"Look at some displays and mingle mostly. There are some panels and meetings, but I think all the forest fire ones were yesterday."*

"Let us know if you see anyone who might be part of the Movement before we do."

"Kind of why I'm here, guys." She lowered her program and caught up with Breeze. They walked past Typhoon with his paper cup of coffee and down to the large room with the trade show vendors. Everything from large-scale timber harvesting equipment to t-shirts reading "Save a tree, hug a forester' were available from booths around the concrete-floored space.

The room wasn't packed; just a few dozen people mostly dressed business casual wandering from display to display. Made it easier to examine the faces Iona passed. So far, none matched any of the known Movement members.

"Do we know how many shapeshifters the Movement has?" Sven asked the van in general. Carlos relayed the same question to Iona through their link.

Cast was the first to answer. "Statistically, they'll have at least a couple, but we don't know for sure."

Byte poked Sven's shoulder. "We have pictures or descriptions of everyone who's visited the Movement's headquarters, but don't know the powers of most of them." Her long braid brushed against his head as she turned towards Cast. "How much longer? I want to get hooked into the convention center's wifi and hack the convention's database."

Cast slowed the van. "It'll go faster once we get past this construction."

A rush of worry flooded from Carlos. Sven tightened his focus to talk directly to him. *"Settle down, even Cast is going to pick up on that. We'll be there in time. See, Iona's doing fine. No bad guys yet."* And Iona was still fine. Maybe in danger of boredom. She was still in the vendor area, examining the material from a training center for firefighters. She fended off the booth attendant's questions and took a pamphlet as she walked away.

Breeze caught up with Iona at a booth displaying tree-planting machinery. "Anything yet?"

Iona held up the pamphlet. "Interesting training course to recommend to the newbies. Seen any old friends?"

"Not yet, but people are still coming in for the big meeting and speeches. Our other friends are on the way, right?"

Sven was pretty sure he didn't imagine the warmness in Iona's manner when she replied, "They're almost here," but he couldn't tell who it was directed towards. He looked out the window for landmarks. The highway sign was legible through the image Iona saw of a banner at the back of a booth selling books on forestry practices.

"We're about to exit the freeway. Be there in ten minutes," he told her.

Sven kept watching what Iona saw while the tech crew tapped furiously on the keyboards. "You guys have pictures of the members we know about? Can we cross reference with the list of conference attendees?"

Byte swatted the back of his head. "Pictures, facial recognition software, secret service list of conference attendees. Just waiting to connect with the conference center and see who's actually shown up."

"Yeah," Teal added. "And patch into their security cameras. Tami, want me to help hack into the center?"

"I've got it." Byte's voice was clipped and short. "You're here to get us into the video feeds. Leave the rest to me."

"Hey," Cast called over his shoulder. "While you two are arguing, does anyone have eyes on Breeze for me?"

Livewire chuckled. "Yeah, I do. He caught up with Typhoon and Flame, then he split off with Typhoon to keep eyes on the registration and entrance areas."

"Thanks. Can you pass word along that I'll be with him as soon as I get us parked?"

"On it."

Sven peered through Iona's view at the road outside the van. "How soon is that going to be?"

Cast peered up at a street sign and took the turn. "Almost there. That's the truck entrance up ahead. Hope they left a spot for us."

Teal whooped. "Got in. One station. Now two stations. Live feeds are just static right now, but they're set up." They leaned over to Byte's station. "Want some help hacking into the secret service or the convention center."

"I said I've got it." Byte tapped in something on her keyboard. "Secret service already gave us their list and we're not quite close enough for the other yet."

The van lurched up into a parking lot, paused for directions from an attendant, and rolled to a stop. Outside the windshield, Sven had a good view of a row of white vans, each with satellite dish and a different television station's logo.

Cast put the van in park and swung his legs around. "I'm on telepath duty now. Someone else work out any parking or camera details." He slid onto the back seat with a blank workstation and slouched down with his eyes closed.

Sven watched as Iona finished her circuit of the vendor hall and wandered over to the exhibit area. *"Anyone interesting in there yet?"*

"Nope. Still looking. Hope you guys have photos out there to match, Roth left town and I'm don't expect Cube to be useful here."

Carlos told her that the techs were setting it up. His emotions were tightly wrapped, but Sven felt the ones that bled through. He was halfway in love with Iona already. After they get through this mission, save the Governor and Vice President, he needed to have a heart-to-heart with Iona and warn her not to break Carlos's heart.

"What?" Carlos whispered, his eyes still closed.

"Nuthin. You guys have the convention database matched up with secret service and the cameras yet?"

Byte turned her monitor so Sven could just see it out the corner of his eye. "I'm ready, just waiting for them to hook into the security link."

Teal grinned and threw their arms up in triumph. "Ta-dah! I'm in. We just checking everyone here with facial recognition?"

Sven gave a thumbs up. "That's the plan. Good job, rookie." He focused inward to tell Iona, but Carlos already had.

Iona asked, *"So, how sure are we that Movement members registered for the convention? They planned that far ahead?"*

Sven took the answer. *"Not sure at all, but it makes sense for them to plant at least a couple in there officially, under whatever names they have the best ID for."*

"It does. No one acting suspicious in here so far."

Sven leaned back, to better watch Carlos and everyone in the back of the van. "What percentage of attendees have shown up?"

Byte flipped to another screen. "Looks like they're over eighty percent right now."

Teal spun their seat sideways. "Security cameras show a hefty line at registration still. Do we know if the VIPs are on site yet?"

Byte had that page too. "Governor arrived a couple of hours ago and reporters interviewed her walking the exhibit floor then. The VP's helicopter is en route from the airport now."

"Guys?" Iona said. *"I'm heading for the registration area. I think I'm being followed. Can you get a match on the cameras? Woman, brown hair in a bun, open blue shirt over a black t-shirt."*

The spike in Carlos's worry matched Sven's as they relayed the request to Teal. Sitting sideways, Sven watched Teal's search through the overlay of what Iona saw inside. He saw the woman following through Iona's eyes before she showed up on the cameras. Just as described, looked like she was in her early twenties.

"I might have it now," Teal said. "This look like her?"

Sven leaned closer to the paused screenshot. "Yep. Run a match."

Iona kept milling around between the registration area and the rooms beyond. Whenever Iona glanced back, the following woman was within line-of-sight. Nothing threatening or sinister about her, but definitely watching Iona.

"Anything yet?" Carlos asked.

"Still working on it," Teal said.

Livewire looked closer at the screen. "When you finish tracing her, Typhoon thinks he recognizes a dude in a navy suit jacket and blue jeans. Dark hair cut short. He'll keep him in sight until you get around to it."

"Almost there. Tell him to keep his shirt on. Flame's follower isn't in our Movement image database, but I'm following up on where the secret service info leads."

Carlos smiled. "Not Movement is a plus."

Cast snorted. "Not in our database isn't the same as not in the Movement."

"Right." Teal turned the screen again. "And the sites of theirs I hacked listed them by codenames, no pictures. But according to the secret service, that is Chloe Andressen. Student at the state university, studying forestry, and an amp on the school wrestling team."

Sven drummed his fingers against his leg. Listed as an amp meant she wasn't a rogue, but that wasn't a guarantee for or against Movement involvement.

Carlos opened his eyes and stared at the screen. "That's her. What kind of power does she have?"

Teal shook their head. "No idea."

Livewire sighed. "Great. One down. Can you search Typhoon's now?"

"Working on it."

"Guys?" Iona said. *"They've announced first call for the auditorium. I'm headed there to get that prime seat I'm supposed to have."*

Breeze and Typhoon announced the same to Cast and Livewire. Cast cleared his throat. "I'll report it. Tagging you all in." His mental voice popped into everyone's head. Sven felt all their presences together – telepaths and the three inside. *"Morrison. We've ID'ed two possible Movement members inside. The team is heading into the big meeting with the VIPs. Any updated instructions?"*

Morrison's voice, projected by Cast, responded. *"No changes. First: Protect the VIPs and the civilians. Second: Capture any Movement members. Third: Keep civilians from seeing your powers. Not necessarily in that order, preferably all of the above."*

Iona was in the first dozen or so people passing the security check into the main presentation hall. She didn't quite make it the seat she'd pre-chosen thanks to some reserved seats for accessibility and reporters, but she ended up closer to the front and center.

Teal's security camera feed had a good view of the metal detectors and double doors into the hall, but not much of the stage or interior of the room. They scrolled between the different television station feeds and left the best two showing the empty stage up on a split screen. Typhoon and Breeze got seats about where they'd planned. None of them had eyes on either of the spotted potential Movement amps and Sven asked Teal and Byte to keep watch on the security screens.

Iona had a clear view of the podium, easy firing range if the speaker was attacked. 'Had' until two big guys sat in front of her.

"Crap," Carlos said. *"Any way to change seats?"*

"Not now. It's filling up and they're trying to hurry it up. Any sign of the one following me?"

"Teal and Byte are watching, haven't seen her yet. Or the one Typhoon saw."

"Is that her?" Teal leaned over to Byte's screen and tapped on it.

"No. Someone with the same shirt. I think the school's forestry students are all wearing matching shirts. And quit messing with my screen." Byte swatted Teal's hand away.

Once the seats in the room were filled, a man wearing a sport coat, jeans, and boots walked on stage to the podium.

Sven watched through Iona's eyes and both television station views on Teal's monitor.

"Welcome everyone to the twenty-fifth annual conference of the Western Forest and Forest Products Association." He paused for light applause. "Before our very illustrious speakers today, I'd like to welcome forestry students from state university and the county community college." More applause. "And some firefighter volunteers from the Bureau of Amplified Human Enforcement. We appreciate your joining the regional forest fire crews."

Several in the audience looked around, more than for the students, but none of the three identified themselves and no one pointed them out. All for the best.

"Now, our speakers for the afternoon, Governor Barb Hosford and Vice President Andrew Stevens."

More applause. The Governor stepped to the podium and spoke about the contributions—current and historical—the forestry industry has made to the state. Sven heard her remarks in triplicate. Luckily, the two screens being recorded played in real-time and matched up with the live speech he heard through Iona's ears.

The camera angles were slightly different, on the one on the left side of Teal's screen Sven could just see the shadows of the state police or secret service officers waiting in the wings. No sign of the two suspected Movement members in the hall or in view of any security cameras. There were too many blind spots there.

The governor finished her speech with her hopes for the future of the industry and the continued safety of those working in it. Then she introduced the Vice President. As Stevens took the podium, the figures in the shadows shifted. Probably the secret service moving closer and the state troopers following the Governor offstage.

One of the shadows moved closer to the edge of the curtain to the right of the VP as he began his remarks. He repeated most of what the Governor said, but couched in terms of benefits to America and American-made products.

The figure in the shadows moved again. At the edge of the curtain now.

"Everyone else seeing this?" Sven asked, pointing at the side of the screen while asking Iona the same.

"Is it secret service watching for threats from the audience?" Byte asked.

The shadow moved again and the spotlight reflected off grey skin.

"That's not an agent," Iona said. Sven felt her rising heartrate through their connection.

Cast added, *"Looks like one of the ones who sprang Roth. Flame, Breeze, Typhoon, anything you can do from in there?"*

"If I get closer maybe," Breeze answered. *"Not from back here."*

"Do we know if wind or water will push the Mist back?" Cast asked.

"No clue," Iona said. *"But they have a way to knock people unconscious."*

On stage, the Vice President kept talking. Mist stepped fully out from behind the curtain and stood behind him like a shadow. People in the first two rows reacted and whispered to each other. The 'click' of a gun's hammer being pulled came through Iona's ears but was too faint for the television cameras to pick up.

Mist put a hand on the Vice President's shoulder and they half turned just as two secret service agents stepped out with guns drawn. "Step away from the Vice President with your hands up."

Mist laughed. "I'm just here to deliver a speech. I apologize for taking up some of the Vice President's time slot, but I'll be brief." They guided the Vice President one step to the side of the podium and took his place at the microphone. "Please don't be alarmed everyone. In the interest in public safety, my associate has removed the bullets from every gun in the building."

One of the agents checked his weapon while the other kept his focused on Mist. Under the stage lights, Mist looked like they were formed of a dense grey cloud. People in the back of the room stood and edged towards the exits, walking in front of the cameras.

"Please remain seated," Mist continued. "To prevent anyone getting hurt in a disorderly evacuation of the room, another associate has locked the doors."

One of the cameras swung around to film the edges of the room where attendees stood, wavering halfway between their seats and the doors.

"Please keep filming," Mist said. "And anyone with a camera on their phone is welcome to take pictures or record. Whatever you like."

An agent rushed Mist. They dissolved into a loose cloud and reformed after he passed. "You won't be able to hurt me, but I can render unconscious anyone who tries. Please wait to one side and no one will get hurt." The same agent feinted and rushed them again. Mist raised one hand in front of his face as he passed and he slumped to the stage. They motioned to the other agent. "Please make him comfortable, I don't think he hit his head, but you should check him over."

The Vice President threw his shoulders back. "We do not negotiate with terrorists."

Mist shook their now solid-looking head. "We are not terrorists. We're just a population devoted to exposing a long-standing government lie."

Cast looked wildly around the van. "Teal, can you shut down those cameras? Block their feeds or something?"

They gestured at the keyboard. "I'm sorry. I only studied how to hack into the feed."

"See if you can figure something out. Morrison has people calling the stations to shut down that end."

On stage, Mist held their arms out soothingly. "Please stay calm. I promise to keep my remarks brief, then your scheduled program will resume."

"Did you feel that?" Iona asked. *"They have someone here who just calmed everyone down. All the nervous energy just left the room."*

Carlos answered. *"Yeah. So besides Mist, they have a mental-empath projector, and a telekinetic or a metal/magnetism manipulator or both."*

Sven repeated Carlos's conclusions to the van. "Check the Movement members we have listed for any of those powers."

Mist lowered their arms as the room fell silent in anticipation. "Like I said, we in the Freedom Movement want to reveal the truth to the public. The government might not actually consider that they lied to you, but they've been concealing facts for decades, isn't that right, Mr. Vice President?"

The Vice President just shook his head.

"Of course, not everyone in the government is in the loop, so to say." Mist gestured down at their body made of smoke. "They've told you all about how Amplified Humans were discovered. All about how we're faster and stronger than the average human. Ten percent stronger and faster. On average. They left out the other powers we have."

"Teal?" Cast asked. "Any luck cutting that feed?"

"No. Still trying."

Mist stepped out from behind the podium and held their arms wide. It seemed a trick of the light at first, but their body faded as the mist dissipated into a soft grey, spreading wide. After enough moments that everyone would believe what they'd seen, it coalesced back into a human form.

Byte raked loose hair back from her face. "Anyone else think we're screwed?"

Teal chuckled without any mirth. "At least we were wrong about this being a kidnapping or murder."

"Small favors," Cast said. "Morrison reports no luck with the media. This is big stuff for them and they want all of it."

The Vice President had edged away from Mist as they reformed. Mist placed a hand on his arm. "Don't worry Mr. Vice President, you're safe here with me. It's an honor to share the stage with you. I didn't vote for your ticket of course." Mist gestured down at their body. "Those of us who are too different don't have all the rights available to most American citizens."

They stepped back behind the podium. "So, the Non-Disclosure Act kept the secrets and was itself kept secret. We say the time has come for Full Disclosure. Full rights to all amps, and to fully inform the American public. Besides those of us who look different, there are amps with mental powers – like my associate who removed the bullets, or another who can send me telepathic updates. We have amps with enhanced senses like the secret service amps with better sight or hearing than average. And there are amps who can manipulate various materials, like metal, water, wind, fire."

Mist stepped out again, this time closer to the front of the stage. "Earlier in the program, you thanked the bureau amps who joined your crews in fighting forest fires. Did anyone wonder how they were so much extra help? I don't know all of the ones here, but wouldn't someone who could direct wind or water be invaluable in putting out a fire. I do know about the power one of the fire fighters has. She starts fires herself and controls them. I'm sure that made it easier to keep the fires for the breaklines in the right place. I even see her here today."

Mist pointed into the audience. Right at Iona. "Iona Sinclair, bureau member for at least five years now."

"Oh, shit," Carlos said at the exact moment Sven did.

CHAPTER TEN

Iona looked wildly around, trying to look like she wasn't the one being singled out. Everyone else was also, but those on either side of her focused on the conference badge on her lanyard. The one with her name in large font and 'National Bureau of Amplified Human Enforcement' below in smaller type. Both of them edged away.

The level of nervous whispers in the crowd rose to a steady murmur. Mist stepped back to the microphone and tapped it twice. "Please, calm down. Bureau amps may be many things, but they use their powers as a public service. It makes me wonder why they've worked so hard to hide those powers for so long."

As Mist spoke, the same calm spread across the room as it had when they started speaking. So, their mental companion was still in the room.

"Guys? Any way to trace that calming back to the source?"

Carlos answered this time, but she could feel them both together. *"Maybe, but only if we're close enough to be affected by the calming. It depends on the skill of the amp doing the calming. Some are subtler than others."*

"So," Mist continued. "All we are asking is that the government and the bureau publicly release the truth about amps. Full Disclosure. We don't want to hurt anybody. We just want all of us to be able to live our lives as full citizens, in full view of our neighbors." They nodded at the Vice President. "Thank you for allowing me to speak, please continue with your remarks, Mr. Vice President. All of the doors are now unlocked."

Mist stepped back from the podium and slowly dissolved into a fine black smoke. The smoke drifted up to the ceiling in a winding tendril.

Conversations erupted immediately. Iona tried to make herself as small as possible, but the seats were close enough that she'd been working to keep from elbowing her neighbors since she sat down. Now she had plenty of elbow room because they'd edged away from her. There were reasons why Full Disclosure was planned for a careful release.

Vice President Stevens stepped to the microphone and shook his head. "I don't know how to follow that."

"Guys? Any suggestions?"

Carlos's presence was soothing, Sven's was deliberate. *"Working on it."*

The Vice President cleared his throat. "So, I'm just going to stick with my prepared speech."

Cast spoke into Iona's mind; his voice was more like listening to a PA in a large room than chatting with Sven and Carlos around a cozy table. *"We've got orders. Don't try and track Mist or any of the others. The surveillance teams will be watching for them. Flame, get out to our van ASAP. Don't answer any questions. Typhoon and Breeze stay casual and monitor crowd reactions inside the room and outside. See what they're saying and what people outside the room already heard."*

The Vice President was talking, but hardly anyone was listening. All around Iona were whispers about Mist's revelations and more than a few stares in her direction. She resisted the urge to look for Typhoon or Breeze and focused on the stage, though she wasn't listening any better than anyone else.

The Vice President was silent for at least a minute before the audience figured out he was done and started a slow wave of applause. Those nearest the doors bolted. The doors opened easily, clearly unlocked.

Iona kept to her seat until everyone else in her row was standing. She shuffled her feet for the slow walk to the end of the row, wishing with every movement that she could leap the chairs and race for the van outside.

The person behind her stayed well back. Her palms warmed and she sucked in deep breaths, holding it in for a five count, and blowing it out slowly. The warmth subsided and she repeated the breathing exercise to keep it down. She shuffled past the last seats in the row and glanced up for the nearest exit. A tall man in uniform, standing eye-to-eye with her, blocked her path.

"Ma'am? I need you to come with me."

Heat flooded into her hands. She clenched them—as if that would stop the fire—and repeated one round of the breathing exercise. "Why?" She was proud of the way her voice didn't shake.

"Whoa," Sven said. *"It's okay. We asked the state police to send one of theirs to escort you out here."*

"A little warning would have been nice."

"Yeah, sorry," Carlos said, *"It's a little frantic in here right now."*

She nodded to the officer and stepped to his side. Her fists stayed tightly balled. Civilians stayed a few feet away, giving them on open circle in which to move. It helped until they were almost to the door when the reporters caught up. Three of them, microphones at their lips and cameras at their backs.

"Ms. Sinclair! Ms. Sinclair!"

"Is what the creature said true?"

"Can you really control fire?"

"Ms. Sinclair, can we have a statement?"

"Have the bureau and government been lying to us all along?"

The trooper sped up his pace and Iona matched his stride. "No comment."

The questions started again. The same ones over and over again. She tightened her balled hands to keep the fire in. The trooper pushed open the door to the outer corridor. "Please stop questioning the agent."

"But is it true?"

Flames spurted out between her fingers. She jerked her left hand away from the trooper.

"Did you do that?" A reporter asked. "Is that your power? Mike, did you get that on camera?"

Shit.

"Flame, keep it together," Sven commanded.

"You can do it, Iona. Breathe and think calming thoughts," Carlos added.

Only the one spurt of flame escaped. Deep breaths in, hold, release. "No comment."

"Good job. You're doing it. Just a little longer to the van."

She smiled at Carlos's encouragement and sent him a mental 'thank you'. Well, sent to both of them. They might be able to shut each other out, but she couldn't.

The trooper pushed open an exit door and let her go ahead of him. That got her away from the reporters inside, but a throng making excited shouts ran over from the main entrance.

"Did you see what happened on stage?"

"What can you tell us? Did it look real?"

"Hey, you're Sinclair. The one the creature named."

Iona walked faster, letting the trooper lead her towards the line of news vans. She kept her head down and focused on her breathing.

The trooper let Iona take the lead. He stayed between her and the incoming reporters. "Stay back. If you saw the video from inside, you know as much as anyone sitting there." He leaned over to Iona. "You know where to meet your team?"

Iona nodded.

"I'll block these bottom feeders, you go on." He let her go on ahead. "People of the press, I may be able to answer some of your questions about what happened inside the convention center today."

More excited questions, most asked over other questions, followed his announcement.

"But, I believe the Vice President will be walking out to his helicopter in just a few minutes. I'll be here later, but this is your only chance to ask him what happened on that stage."

Iona glanced back. All the reporters and cameras were rushing back to the building. The trooper smiled and raised a thumb's up.

"Thanks." She sketched a half-wave and dashed to the only white van without a station or network logo. Ten feet away and the back doors swung open.

Sven reached out a hand. "Want a ride?"

Carlos added, "Or a seat?" The back of the van had six seats mounted at computer consoles, three per side.

"One of each, please." She reached out for the van, but pulled her hands back. Burning up the van wouldn't help anyone.

The guys reached for her.

"Not the hands."

Sven grinned. "Of course not." He closed his hand around her right bicep and Carlos the left. Together, they pulled her the short distance up into the van.

"Welcome aboard," Cast called from the driver's seat. "Buckle up everyone. We've got our orders. Keep an eye on the news feeds and any media you can." Livewire was in the passenger seat, Teal and Byte each sat at a workstation.

Sven and Carlos sat at the back two consoles on the right side. Iona buckled into the center seat on the left side. "How much got out?"

Cast groaned. "Every bit of it." He eased the van out of its parking space and exited the parking lot.

"Shit." She pressed into the seat back, keeping her palms from touching anything. At least it felt safe inside. Surprisingly safe. To her right, Byte worked a keyboard, switching the monitor between three different four-way views. Two of them were live 'breaking news' accounts with a banner along the bottom of the screen reading 'Mysterious Being Claims Government Coverup: Truth or Hoax?'.

Plenty to worry about there. And more with the next screen showing her face. Shit and more shit. None of it disturbed her feeling of safety.

"Are you guys doing this to me? Making me feel safe?"

Sven answered. *"Not in our skillset. Maybe having us around is comforting."* She swore there was a smile in his mental voice.

Carlos added, *"It's probably just being in here, out of the public eye. Are your hands okay?"*

"How are you on time?" Sven asked, concern coloring his thoughts.

She shook them out. The fire that threatened inside was at bay now. Nice, safe, van. *"Time's fine. The stress of getting past all them was a bit of a worry, but all good now."*

Carlos gave Sven a funny look and Iona realized that, as close as the two of them were, Sven hadn't told Carlos about the remedy to her control problem. Or maybe not about her problem at all.

From the back of the van, she couldn't see much of the road outside, but soon they reached highway speeds. They'd reach the bureau soon.

"Shit." Cast pulled the van sharply to the right, onto an exit ramp. "Sorry, boys and girls and others. Reports of a crowd of reporters and protestors outside the office. We have to take a back way in. I'm pulling off up here. Someone find the heating and cooling repair stickers back there. As soon as I stop, hop out and slap one on each side."

Teal grabbed two rolls of vinyl from the rack overhead. The van lurched to a stop and Sven flung open the door and accepted one of the rolls from Teal. They both hopped down and disappeared past the doors. Two thumps on one side and three on the other and they both hopped back in and pulled the doors closed. "Ready, Cast."

Cast threw the van into reverse before Sven and Teal were in their seats. Iona caught Teal's arm and swung them back into their seat. Carlos did the same for Sven.

Byte switched tabs on her screen. "Ours isn't the only office with a crowd. The D.C. office has the biggest protest. We're second largest since the news came down here, but most major cities have something. All offices are on lockdown and all phenos are asked to stay in their compound or in the offices for everyone's safety."

Teal snorted. "Gator's going to love that."

Cast swung the van back onto the highway. "She's getting reamed out by DC now, along with Morrison and Manik. Seems we were supposed to have known what the Movement's real plans were today."

Iona's own face appears on one of the screens.

"And you, Flame, are going down in the history books just like Edward Muncie."

Iona swiveled her seat so it faced front instead the monitor. "And remember how well that went for him. Lost all his weight lifting medals and died during the testing of his powers. First identified amp. Big whoop."

Cast floored the van. "That's why you're staying out of sight back there. We'll be there in ten minutes or less."

"You doing okay? Staying calm and non-flammable?" Sven asked. He sat with his back to the monitors on his side of the van.

She shook out her hands and held them palms up. *"All good. See – no fire."* She kept them held out until the van plunged down the ramp into the back garage entrance.

Cast parked the van. "Home again kids. Morrison wants us to join them. Infirmary level meeting room. ASAP."

Byte tapped away at her keyboard. "Okay, everything here is uploaded."

Carlos opened the back doors and they filed out. The stairs were closer than the elevator, and less likely to get them noticed. The fire was at bay, but Iona avoided touching handrails or doors just in case. Shouted conversations spilled out as soon as the conference room door was opened. Sven was the only one big enough to hide Iona so she followed him closely inside.

Morrison stopped mid-sentence. "Here's most of the team that had to deal with surveillance's screw up."

Livewire looked around the room. "Typhoon and Breeze weren't ID'ed. They stayed behind to gauge crowd reactions."

Morrison sighed. "The VIPs and civilians are safe. Movement perps escaped best as we can tell. Tech and med teams are working out a way to capture and contain Mist if we ever get another chance. DC is working on an official response they want to announce in the next couple of days. Until then, we're to monitor all online feeds, keep up surveillance on the Movement, and Flame needs to keep out of the public eye. Left and Right will go with her. Leave when we're done here, pick a safe house, and tell no one which one you pick. I'll contact you when it's safe to return."

"Exile. Great. Sorry to drag you two with me."

Carlos projected an air of ease. *"Not your fault. We can call it a company-paid vacation."*

"I like it," Sven said. *"How long will it take for you run home for our go bags? Mine's on my closet floor. Twenty minutes or so? Iona, can you be ready by then? I'll make sure we have groceries where we're going."*

Gator was talking now. Warning about the impact this would have on phenos short term and long term. Asking for extra consideration for the bureau phenos who might be stuck in the offices for a few days.

"Twenty maybe. After they release us here. Thirty at the outside."

Manik made a few comments that echoed Gator. Iona checked the room for Lisa. Would these new guidelines even affect her invisible boyfriend? She was over on the other side of the room, but there were too many others in the way for them to make eye contact.

Morrison checked his phone and let it clatter onto the table. "We're just going in circles now. Let's break. Keep a watch on the Movement's online activity and the public's reaction to today. Everyone keep their heads down out there – especially Flame. I don't want any new photos of you to surface."

Last to enter meant first to leave. Iona and Carlos darted out. He walked with her as far as the turn to the elevators. He brushed a lock of her hair over her shoulder. "Maybe find a hat to wear."

She smiled. "I have something better in mind. See you in twenty." She felt the impression of his touch even after entering her room. Her 'something better' involved a tube of temporary hair dye she'd bought for a mission and hadn't needed. Ten minutes to make her hair not its easily identifiable red. The eighteen hour limit wasn't up yet, but would be before they reached most of the safe houses, so that was something else she should take care of.

By design, her go bag contained only things for two or three days. She added enough clothes for a few more, and, for Carlos, her favorite tweed newsboy cap – the one that slightly clashed with her red hair but would be perfect with the darker brunette that the dye should turn her hair.

The dye was in the bathroom where she thought she'd seen it last. She whipped off her t-shirt and tossed it in the direction of her bed. Following directions, she mixed the two tubes together and applied it to her hair. While she waited the ten minutes, she removed the rest of her clothes and took her waterproof vibrator and sat on the seat integrated into the corner of the shower. Just one 'perk' of living in the infirmary.

She leaned back into the corner and called up the imaginary hands she used to set the mood, but they refused to be anonymous. Carlos's touch on her shoulder and his sweet shy smile took the place of one pair of hands and Sven's sparkling eyes and easy laugh were the other. Her personal rule about dating co-workers was straining. And the decent human rule about not messing up a pair of best friends was in trouble too.

Thoughts like that had to be shut down or she'd never be ready in time. She let the imaginary hands be non-anonymous just this once for the sake of speed. One set of hands stroked her breasts from the sides, firm thumbs running over both nipples until they hardened. Imaginary lips belonging to that set of hands pressed kisses up the side of her neck. She arched her head back with eyes closed to avoid those sparkling blue eyes she knew were part of the hand-and-lip package.

Another set of imaginary hands trailed feather-light touches from her hip bones around to her inner thighs, igniting her senses and causing her hips to raise off the seat. Teasingly, those fingers stayed on the soft skin of her upper thighs, just tickling the edges of the hair over her triangle. Keeping eyes closed to avoid that imaginary sweet smile attached to those feather-soft fingers, she stroked the vibrator from where those fingers left off and towards her center.

The imaginary kisses on her throat drifted down to join the thumbs on her left breast and her breath caught, then panted in time with her vibrator strokes. She let the imaginary touches keep pace with the vibrator until climax rocked through her body.

With a sigh of regret for how letting these imaginary hands match up with too-familiar eyes and smiles was going to affect her the next time she tried to rein them in, she checked the time. The dye on her hair was just past the time it needed, but should be fine.

The color darkened the rinse water as it swirled down the drain. She rinsed as long as she dared and toweled off quickly. The resulting color wasn't super dark, but the red was suitably disguised. Twenty minutes had passed, but neither Carlos nor Sven had called in telepathically or on her phone. They'd just have to wait for her to toss on jeans and a shirt if they called now.

She made it as far as jeans and a bra before her phone chirped with a text message. It wasn't from the guys but from her grandpa Paul up in Canada. News traveled fast, he was worried about her.

Still shirtless, she took the time to tap out a reply: 'Managing okay here. Going off the grid for a bit. Love you.' He could spread the word to the rest of her family. She got the purple t-shirt on before the next text. This one from Carlos: 'Just parking now. Blue car beside the east stairs.'

A thumbs' up icon was the fastest possible reply as she flipped the hair up and pulled the cap over it and grabbed her go bag and tablet. 'Off-grid' meant no internet, but she had plenty of reading material already loaded.

With a sigh, she switched off the lights as she left her phone on the desk. Forced out of her home because of her powers: Round Two. And just how lame was her life that an infirmary-level room was 'home'?

Her denim duffle bag was awfully light for an unknown number of days away. A quick, undetected walk to the staircase would be appropriate. Instead, Morrison stood on guard halfway between the conference room and the door to the garage stairway.

"All set then?" he asked.

She tried to look confident. "I think so. I left my phone."

"Good. I've left instructions for your room to be sealed until you return. Think of this as a nice all-expenses-paid vacation to a place not of your choosing."

"One way to look at it. Do you know where we'll be?"

He shook his head. "No and I don't want to know. Your companions are choosing. It's one of the bureau's properties, but there are dozens within a half-day's drive."

"What's going to happen here?"

He sighed, a deep sigh that shook his entire six and a half foot frame. "DC has taken charge. They'll decide on the official response and make the announcement. Your guess is as good as mine for when they'll reach a decision."

"Are you saying I should have packed more?" The duffle bag was suddenly far too light.

He chuckled. "Entirely up to you. Keep your head down as you drive through town, but that hat should help." He cocked his head to one side. "And the brunette is a nice look on you."

"Probably not keeping it. See you when you call us in." She flipped her hand in a half-wave and marched past him to the garage stairs. Carlos waited at his little blue hatchback just beyond the door into the second parking level.

She reached the passenger door in five steps. "We all set?"

His smile sparkled. "I like the hat." He opened the trunk and she tossed her bag in beside two others and a plastic cooler with a faded blue lid. "We're just waiting on Sven."

"Has he already called shotgun?"

He shook his head and opened the back door. "He hasn't, but you're in the back with your head down. Sit in the middle, away from the windows."

"Shall I slouch and stare at my missing phone, too?"

"Good idea." He grinned, so she knew he was at least partly joking. "At least when we pass other cars." He leaned closer to her. He smelled like soap and sandalwood. "You changed your hair color? That was fast."

"Temporary color. It'll fade over the next week or so. I brought more in case I need to do it again." She slid into the seat and buckled the belt.

"Good idea. Ah, the slowpoke is almost here." Carlos climbed into the driver's seat and closed his door just as the stairway door opened to let Sven out onto the garage floor.

The brighter lights from the stairwell backlit him, throwing his broad-shouldered frame into silhouette. As the door closed, its small square window lit his blond hair like a halo. He slid into the passenger seat, dragging in a laptop bag and small backpack with him.

"Onward."

Carlos started the car and looked at Sven until Sven buckled his seat belt. "Okay. Now we can go. Everyone ready?"

Sven finger-combed his hair. "Our grocery order is ready for pickup now. It should be on the way."

Should? "Don't you know where we're going?" she asked.

"Uh-uh," Carlos answered for him, "Only the driver knows. I've been keeping my head full of song lyrics just in case someone is trying to tap in and listen for our destination."

"So you're not telling me either." She said it as a statement, but hoped Carlos might tell her.

"Nope. No one knows. I marked nine or ten sites reserved so if someone here wants to find us without a lot of searching, they'll have to contact one of us first. I picked sites within a four-hour drive in all directions."

Carlos stopped the car at the garage exit under the neighboring block. No reporters were visible on the sidewalk and he eased out into traffic. "Our regular store?"

"No – the one off the freeway."

"You guessed the right direction."

Carlos headed for the westward on-ramp. They pulled off the freeway two exits later and almost directly into the store's parking lot. Specially marked parking spaces near the doors were for grocery pickup. Sven hopped out as soon as Carlos put the car in park. "Pop the back and sit tight, okay?"

Iona grabbed a book from her bag, pulled her knees up, and rounded her shoulders to read. With luck, she'd look like a teenaged sister waiting for her big brother to finish his errands. As long as no one looked too closely. Been a long time since she could actually pass for a teen.

Various thumps and bumps from behind her seat heralded the stowing of groceries and sundries. "What'd he order? Good stuff, I hope."

Carlos turned so his profile was clear. "No idea. He's pretty good at planning, so we should be okay. If supplies run low, I can forage for more."

"That remote, huh?"

"Not completely uncivilized, but a ways out there."

The trunk slammed closed and Sven slipped back into his seat. "All set. Onward."

Carlos started the car. "What's wrong?"

"Nothing."

"And yet you're disappointed."

Sven sighed. "It's dumb. I had a line ready if anyone asks where we're going. Or why we're loading up on supplies. And they didn't ask."

Iona chuckled. "So tell us the story you have for us. We might as well all use the same one."

Sven twisted so he could see both her and Carlos. "That me and my cousin," He gestured in her direction, "are heading to visit our grandparents at their vacation house. And, this year, I'm bringing my boyfriend to meet them."

Carlos laughed. "Glad I knew about the plan before you told strangers. Otherwise, I might not have sold it." He drove out of the parking lot and onto the road leading back to the freeway. "Settle in and get comfortable." He switched on the radio. From the song, it was one of the pop music stations. When the DJ started her beginning of drive-time patter after the song, Iona knew which one it was. She usually flipped between three different stations and a streaming service.

The DJ kept talking, "And today, our local news went global. People claiming to be from a group of Amplified Humans called the Freedom Movement took over Vice President Steven's speech at the Forestry Association event at the convention center. Officials are still trying to find these amps and confirm their announcements of hidden powers that they claim all amps possess. The Bureau of Amplified Human Resources is assisting law enforcement in finding these amps, but have offered no formal statement. Weather and traffic after these messages."

Iona blew out a sigh. "So much for keeping this under the radar."

Sven turned the radio down. "At least they didn't mention you. Or that any amps were identified with their power."

"Yet." She slumped down in the seat. "Sorry you two are getting stuck with me in hiding."

"Are you kidding?" Sven asked. "An extra paid vacation. Lodging, food, and gas all provided by the bureau."

"What he said," Carlos added and they merged onto the freeway. "Besides, it's only until this either blows over or they go ahead with disclosure."

"You really think that's what'll happen? After all these years about talking about it?"

Sven waved at the radio. "They didn't mention it, but it's all over the internet and regular news stations will be blasting it until the next big event. The bureau can't suppress it anymore."

Late afternoon traffic was as heavy as usual for a Friday with people leaving work early for the weekend. It wasn't long before any semblance of suburbia had fallen behind and they drove west through a mix of farmland and forest.

The sun was ahead of them. Not low enough yet to be in Carlos's eyes, but that might get to be a problem later. "Should I have packed beach wear?"

Sven answered. "Since it's the same as what you'd wear in the mountains or town, I hope so." She couldn't see his face, but there was a smile in his voice. "Hope you brought a swimsuit though. Some of the safehouses have hot tubs."

Carlos braked as the truck in front of them suddenly flashed its turn signal and stopped. "If you required certain amenities, you should have said something sooner. Distance from town and a peaceful atmosphere were my choices."

"Video game console?" Sven's voice tilted up hopefully. Static rippled through the music on the radio. "Or a satellite station."

"Sorry." Carlos shook his head. "Nothing trackable onboard. You'll have to entertain us with your sparkling wit."

Sven ducked forward and straightened again, and snapped a sheet of paper. "I came prepared." He glanced back at Iona. "For both of you. I brought a list of questions to help people get to know each other. Since we're going to be spending some time in close quarters, I thought it might help."

"Mother's maiden name, first pet, and childhood address?" Iona guessed.

"And email password." Sven twisted in his seat so one shoulder was against the seat back and his profile was backlit against the windshield. "I'll ask, take turns answering and say the first thing that comes to mind. Don't think too hard about it."

Iona looked at the rear view mirror to see if she could see Carlos's reaction. He might have been doing the same because their eyes met. He tilted his head questioningly so she nodded. He nodded back.

She slipped off both shoes and pulled her feet up to sit cross-legged. "Okay. Go ahead."

Sven shook his paper for dramatic effect and held it up as if it were an ancient scroll. "If you could have dinner with anyone in the world, who would it be?"

"Is language an issue?" Iona asked.

"Living person, or anyone ever?" Carlos asked.

Sven sighed. "Assume you know the same languages and sure, anyone from any time in history."

Carlos tapped his fingers against the steering wheel. "Someone who helped build the stone circles and can explain what they were for."

"I was going to say that famous chef who gives restaurant tours, but your answer is better."

"Sven flicked his paper again. "Next question."

"Wait a minute," Carlos said. "You have to answer, too."

Iona agreed. "If we're all going to be in this cabin or whatever, we all have to answer."

"Okay then. The singer/actress Natalie Kitur. Next: Would you like to be famous and for what?"

Iona shuddered. "I've had enough fame already. None for me."

Carlos met her eyes via the rearview mirror. "Good point. I'd take fame, but not like that. Only if I were actually good at performing or sports. Music maybe."

"Same for me," Sven said. "Having my name known for some accomplishments, but not my face. It'd suck to not be able to go to the store or the movies without being bothered. Okay. If you're shipwrecked alone on a deserted island, what one book would you want to have with you?"

Carlos answered immediately. "The Bible."

"How come?" Iona asked.

"I told my mom I'd read the whole thing someday. And I know I wouldn't be there long. He'd know where I was and bring a ship or helicopter to get me."

Sven's shoulders shifted against his seat. "I, uh, didn't think of that. This question doesn't mean as much for us. I'd want a book of blank pages and enough pens or pencils to last until he brought a rescue. Iona, what about you?"

She snorted. "I'd want the biggest, most complete book on survival skills I could find."

Both guys chuckled and Carlos asked, "Can I change my answer?"

She didn't kick his seat. "You two can just call on each other to look up facts and instructions while you're setting up transportation."

"As long as we're both alive and conscious," Sven said. "Our link doesn't work so well otherwise."

Carlos moved into the right lane for a sports car to zip past them as the road hit a steeper patch. "Except for dreaming."

"Right." Sven nodded. "Except for dream sharing."

Iona thought about some of the dreams she remembered. "I can't decide if that's cool or creepy."

"You get used to it. Next question: When you have to call someone, do you rehearse what you're going to say first? Nope, I never do. Carlos?"

"Usually. Iona?"

"Sometimes, I guess? If it's a business call to someone I don't know."

"Okay." Sven shook out his paper. "In two minutes or less, what would be a perfect day for you?"

"Me first," Iona said, staring out the front window, her view framed by blond hair on the right and dark hair on the left. "Sleeping late wearing cozy flannel pajamas. Breakfast is a smoked salmon omelet with a side of French toast. After breakfast, take a short hike through shady woodland trails with friends. Late afternoon, hot chocolate and marshmallows around a fire. And later, just sitting around with fancy cocktails, good music low enough for conversation and loud enough to hear."

The lane they were in ended as the road was back to single lanes in each direction. Still steadily uphill and a light rain misted the windshield.

"Sounds nice." Carlos switched on the wipers. "I agree with sleeping in. But then I want a sunny beach with a warm ocean and a light breeze. A book to read in the shade in between body surfing runs. Mangos and pineapple for breakfast, fish tacos for lunch, and my mom's tamales for dinner."

Iona considered. "Is that a clue about where we're heading? West to the ocean, then south until the water's warm?"

"That's a lot of south," Sven said with yet another rattle of his paper. "You're both in charge of meal planning. Just tell me what to prep and how to cook it. My perfect day would be one where I spent half the day burrowed away by myself and the rest surrounded by friends, ending with a night of passion with someone I loved. Next: When did you last sing to yourself and when to someone else?"

Iona did kick his seat. "What kind of questions are these? I don't sing where anyone can hear me. I sang along with the radio the other day."

Carlos held up one finger. "In the shower this morning." He added a second finger. "I sang at you last night on our way home from work."

"Yeah, you did. Keep your day job. I think the last time I sang to myself was when I vacuumed last weekend. And I went out for karaoke a few weeks ago." He rattled the paper again. The rain stopped and Carlos switched off the wipers. "If you lived to be ninety, would you rather have the mind or the body of a thirty-year-old for the last sixty years of your life?"

"Body," Carlos answered promptly. "No Alzheimer's or senility in my family."

"Same for me," Iona said.

Sven cocked his head to one side, his hair just long enough to sway. "I'm going to hope my amp-ness keeps my body going and wish for the mind of a thirty-year-old. As long as I keep anything I learn after that. Next question."

He didn't ask the question. The car's engine and the wind passing outside were the only sounds until Carlos asked, "Is that a pause to build suspense?"

Sven shook his head. "Sorry, it just threw me for a minute. Do you have a premonition about how you'll die? That's a nope from me."

"Me too," Carlos said.

Iona stared out the side window at the forest rushing past. "I've never really thought about it, so no. If I had to think about it, I'd guess fire would be involved."

That brought the mood down, but Sven picked right back up with the questions, sometimes giving his own answer right after the question and sometimes letting someone else answer first. The questions, and the order, seemed familiar, but she couldn't think of why. As often as Carlos's and Sven's answers didn't match up, Iona still saw a lot of similarities in the men. Both were empathetic, caring, and had a sense of humor about themselves. This exile was going to be a complete test of her dating rule. Either one of them would be perfect for her if she didn't work with them. That only left the problem of which one.

More familiar questions – Share a positive quality about the others, how close is your family? – finally triggered Iona's memory. "These questions. I've seen this list before."

Sven dropped the paper low so she couldn't see the top of it over his shoulder. "They're on the internet, so you could have seen them."

"Uh-huh. Want to tell Carlos the title of the page or should I?"

Sven didn't answer. Carlos looked over at him with a grin. "Looks like you're going to have to tell me."

She leaned forward. "When I saw it, it was '36 questions to make you fall in love.' You were supposed to read the questions and answer them sitting across from someone and make eye contact while you answer.

Supposedly, it makes you fall in love. Why do you suppose Sven chose this list?" There, let Sven squirm. The car ride made it impossible for eye contact, but their answers did reveal more than they'd already known about each other.

"Really?" Carlos asked. "Did you doubt our love for you?"

Sven reached an arm over the center console and patted Carlos on the thigh. "Never. They seemed like good getting-to-know-each-other questions since Iona doesn't know us as well as we know each other. And we might be stuck together for a week or three. And she's single. And you're single."

Carlos patted Sven's hand. "You're single, too." His hand slid off Sven's and returned to the steering wheel.

Sven's hand returned to his seat.

Iona waited, but neither of them spoke for several minutes. "Are you two telepathing about me?"

"Yes."

"No."

She slumped back in her seat. "That's reassuring." Given her history with them both, she was inclined to believe Carlos's 'yes'. He seemed incapable of lying. At least to her.

"We were talking about us," Sven said.

Carlos's head turned to Sven and back to the road. "He was trying to explain why I should ask you out even though he likes you."

"Too," Sven said, turning towards Carlos. "I like you, too. Because he does."

Sigh. "So the whole time we're holed up together, we're supposed to figure out which one of you I'm supposed to date?" Glancing out the window wasn't any help. "It doesn't look like we'll have any place to go out to." The car slowed and Carlos turned it onto a side road with a weathered sign she couldn't read in the fading sunset. "Are you pulling over?"

He looked up at the rear view mirror and she met his smiling eyes. "This is the way. Honest. We're almost there. And any dating or not dating won't be happening out here. It depends on how the media handles this, but you'll need to stay out of public places."

The road wound through thick forest that completely shaded the road. The bits of sky she glimpsed overhead were darkening with twilight. Driveways, mostly gravel, appeared now and then to either side of the road, but visible houses at the ends of those driveways were few and far between.

Signs warning of lower speed zones ahead were a welcome sign of civilization. After the headlights hit the third one, the forest thinned and the lights from houses were visible at the ends of shorter, but still gravel, driveways. An actual road intersected, then another, and then they reached what might be called a town.

"According to the map, this is the closest shopping we'll have." Carlos took a hand from the steering wheel to wave it left and right. "If we need anything else, we have to head to highway 101."

"How far is that?" Sven asked.

Carlos returned his hand to the wheel and stopped at a stop sign. "Forty-five minutes or so. Each way."

For a first look at her sanctuary, or prison depending on how you looked at it, Iona wasn't impressed. A gas station shared a building with a grocery store. Another building was divided into a café and a tavern. A tiny shop beside that advertised books over one door and antiques over another. And the lot opposite appeared to be both auto repair and junkyard.

She relaxed back into the seat. "Let's hope your supplies hold out then."

Carlos chuckled. "We got plenty. In the morning, I'll come back here and fill the tank. I don't want to be caught without enough for a getaway."

"We could stop now," Iona suggested

"Nah. I want to unpack before it gets any darker."

Sven twisted to look at her. "And I'd rather keep you out of sight as much as possible."

She blew out a breath. "Good thing I like to play hermit once in a while."

Sven chuckled. "But are you really a hermit when you're with other people?"

She was still figuring out the best retort when Carlos flung the car around a corner.

"Sorry. Almost missed the turn."

The turn onto a road with no identifying sign, no lights, and if there was striping to divide the lanes it had faded down to nothing. "This isn't a horror movie setting is it?" She looked to the rear view mirror to see Carlos as he answered.

He met her eyes. "Probably not. It's a bureau cabin, though. Who knows what's gone on there before? Anyone around here asks, it belongs to his aunt." He jerked his head Sven-ward.

"Why mine?"

"Just in case they prefer blonds to people like me up here."

Iona sighed. "You couldn't find a safe house in a town that appreciated diversity?"

"Did the best I could. Don't distract me, I'm counting driveways."

She tried to count along, but didn't know when he'd started or what number he was looking for. All light was gone now except their headlights and the occasional lights filtering through the trees from a distant house.

They curved up another rise and one steep hill before Carlos made a triumphant noise and eased his car onto a driveway with a house number on a post to the right and a tall tree to the left. The driveway wound this way and that around more huge trees until the headlights finally illuminated a cute log cabin with a covered porch along the front.

"Really?" Iona asked. "You couldn't find a straw house in a wheat field?"

Sven twisted around again. "We're not hiding from the big bad wolf."

"Yeah, but putting a firestarter in a log cabin surrounded by forest doesn't sound like the best idea. Isn't there a brick house in an abandoned quarry somewhere?"

Carlos put the car in park and switched off the engine. "They'll be less likely to expect you up here. Wait here while I get the lights on."

Carlos left them alone in the car. Sven unbuckled his seat belt and turned to face her again. "Sorry if I made you uncomfortable by trying to get some flirting going. He deserves someone special."

"Thank you for thinking I'm special, I guess."

"Is there a possibility that you might like him?"

She kept her eyes on the cabin. Carlos was inside now and carriage lamps lit up on each side of the door. "I told you about my policy to not date co-workers."

"It's not like the bureau doesn't encourage us to date. Or at least make little amp babies."

She snort-laughed. "Maybe that's why I made that rule. I don't want to play into their hands. And I really don't want to raise a baby firestarter. Can you just imagine?"

He made a horrified face. "And I thought little mind readers would be a terror." His mouth relaxed into an easy grin. "But if you ever decide to change your mind, you could do a lot worse than our friend out there."

"Pretty sure I've dated all kinds of 'worse' already."

"We'll have plenty of time to swap bad date stories."

She looked past Sven to the door of the cabin. "He's waving us in. Must be safe inside."

They each grabbed their own bag. Sven sent her inside first so he could guard the rear. Guard it from owls, bats, and mosquitos, she supposed. All the sounds came from the dark branches overhead. Inside, the cabin was bright and inviting. It was rustic, walls and floor of wood polished to a bright sheen, and furniture made of joined timbers.

The stone fireplace dominated the wall to the right, a basket of kindling and logs beside it. A kitchen with a dining table filled the space across from the door and a hallway led off to the left.

Iona lifted her bag slightly. "Where's my room?"

"Down the hall," Carlos answered. "There's two of them. One for you and one for us."

She followed the hallway and looked in each of the four doors. Bathroom, linen closet, bedroom with two beds, and bedroom with one bed. She tossed her duffle beside the bed all by itself. All alone. Just like her. A king-size bed, she noted. The other two beds were much smaller. If she had to be exiled, at least she'd be comfortable.

The guys were inspecting the kitchen. "Everything seems to work in here," Sven said. "The pantry is loaded with canned goods and the fridge smells clean. Want to get the first load of food from the trunk?"

At least she could always trust them to not talk about her as soon as she left the room. Not when they could talk about her when she was right there. The porch lights made twin circles on the porch that encompassed the three-step staircase down to where the car sat. Opening the car door to pop the trunk latch added another spot of electric light in the dark forest.

A car's engine—more likely a truck's—interrupted the night's silence. Their cabin was well back from the road, but sound echoed off all the trees, making distance impossible to judge. All the food and supplies filled the trunk, it was going to take several trips to get it all inside. Things in the cooler needed to get in first, but it was blocked in by a solid mass of filled grocery bags.

Lights from behind flooded the trunk with light and that truck's engine was coming closer.

She concentrated her thoughts. "Uh guys? Are you listening right now? We've got a visitor." She turned to face the approaching headlights, holding one hand up to shield her eyes. Sprinting inside would only arouse suspicion, questions at least. The vehicle – pretty sure it was a Jeep – slowed as it got closer and stopped some twenty feet behind Carlos's car.

"Got you." Sven's voice sounded in her head. *"We're linked and watching from in here."*

"Unless you want us to come out there," Carlos added.

".Just stay there until we see who this is."

A man climbed out of the Jeep and left the door open and engine running. "Hi there." He stepped around his open door and walked half the distance to her. A black lab-looking dog hopped out of the Jeep and snuffled around. "I'm Bill Dupree. My cabin is a few miles further up the road. I'm sort of an unofficial neighborhood watch around here. Are you the owner of this place or a weekend renter?"

"I'm here with some friends from college. The cabin belongs to one of their aunts and she's letting us vacation here for a week or so."

The dog cocked a leg at the base of a bush beside the driveway and kept sniffing his way closer to Iona.

"Okay if I give you my card for her? I'd like to let all the cabin owners know I drive through once a week or so. Always on a different day, of course. Just to make sure there's no one here who shouldn't be. With the recent news, I'm watching out for amps who might be fleeing the city."

"Why's that?"

He snorted. "How'd you manage to miss the news? It's on everything."

"We've been driving for a couple of days and haven't seen a TV." She stayed out of the lamplight, hoping he wouldn't recognize her. That television shot was mostly her red hair and it was gone for now.

"They've lied to us for decades." He pounded his fist against his palm. "The amps, the government, their damn bureau. Amps have got more powers than we were told. They could take over everything." His dog had been zigzagging across the driveway and reached Iona, his tail wagging.

She reached out a hand for the dog to sniff. He swiped his tongue across the back of her hand and leaned his head against her leg.

"Looks like Rex likes you."

Need to get rid of him. *"Anything you guys can do to encourage him to leave?"* She rubbed Rex's head with her knuckles. "I love dogs. Can't have one in my apartment, though."

Sven's voice, backed by Carlos's power answered, *"Wish we could make him think he left the water running at home. Unless tossing a pinecone at his car would get him going, we've got nothing."*

"He's my hunting buddy. And he's trained to detect amps. Never misses."

"Uh, that's impressive."

He reached into his coat pocket and pulled out a thin case. "Take one of my cards for your friend's aunt. I like to let folks know that I'm keeping an eye on the cabins up here when they're vacant." He slid a card free from the case.

Iona had to nudge Rex out of the way to reach for the card. She kept her face angled down at the dog and one hand on his head. "Thanks. I'll make sure she knows." The card had a cartoon of a house's roof on one side and 'Dupree Roofing' emblazoned across the top.

He called Rex with one sharp short whistle. Rex rubbed his head against Iona's hand and bounded to the Jeep and inside. "Enjoy your stay here." He pulled his door closed and revved the engine as he reversed the Jeep into a three-point turn to head back out the driveway.

She grabbed two bags of groceries. *"Did you get all of that?"*

Sven passed her in the doorway. "We did. I don't think he's as good at training dogs as he thinks he is." He hefted the cooler and followed her inside. "I guess this gives us an 'average citizen's' view of full disclosure."

Carlos was right on Sven's heels. "The average back-woods yokel's view anyway." Carlos shook his head. "His emotions didn't give away much. He didn't recognize you at all. He's what he seems – a good ol' boy trying to be a big deal in the neighborhood by playing neighborhood watch."

One more trip from each of them and all the supplies were inside and the door locked. She tried to help put away the groceries, but Carlos and Sven had such perfect coordination and choreography in the narrow space that she left them to it and searched the linen closet for sheets and blankets for all three beds.

She did her bed last so she could flop back when it was done. This had been one long-ass day. Thankfully, the bed was comfortable, but she'd be able to sleep even if it was mediocre. A growl from her stomach reminded her that 'lunch' was a few rushed snacks here and there. Some of the groceries they'd unloaded should be turned into dinner.

It didn't take more than a couple of steps out of her room to smell that the guys had already started cooking.

"That smells amazing. What is it and is there enough for me?"

Sven was at the stove, stirring something in a skillet. "This is chicken fettucine, but you're smelling the roasted Brussel sprouts."

Her nose wrinkled at the name and Sven laughed.

"You'll like these. They have maple syrup, brown sugar, and bacon."

"Okay. I'll try them, but I reserve the right to just pick out the bacon."

Carlos sidled past her to gather plates from a cupboard. "He didn't like them either the first time I made them. You'll see." He set the plates between flatware already on the table. "If you want something other than water to drink, see if there's something in the fridge you like."

"Water's fine." She checked the two cupboards she was blocking and found glasses to fill at the sink.

Sven followed her with the skillet and ladled out equal piles of creamy noodles onto each plate. Carlos grabbed a pan from the oven, releasing a mingled sweet, savory, toasty aroma that came to the table with him so he could add the vegetables to the plates.

Iona sat in the seat opposite the kitchen. "I guess it's my turn for the dishes since you both cooked."

They took their seats, Carlos across from her and Sven to her right. Carlos raised his glass to her. "Not tonight. You had the longest day. We'll wash up and let you have it tomorrow."

"Thank you. And I'm impressed at the culinary excellence here."

Sven chuckled. "'Excellence' is pushing it. We're not helpless in the kitchen, but there's a few things we each do really well."

It smelled amazing, but still, Brussel sprouts? She stabbed a square of bacon from up against one of the green orbs and sighed with rapture when it hit her taste buds. Sweet, salty, and smoky all wrapped up together. If the gross little cabbages tasted even half this good, she'd change her mind about them.

To be on the safe side, she chose one of the smaller ones, and stabbed it with a piece of bacon. The salty/smoky/sweet flavors dominated the sharp greenness. "Fine, you win. These are delicious." She looked from one to the other. "If I praise your cooking enough, does that mean you'll cook every night?"

Sven waved his empty fork in her direction. "Not a chance. You cook night after next."

The pasta was every bit as good as the vegetables and she cleaned her plate. "I'm full, but did we bring anything for dessert?"

Carlos answered, "Bags and bags of cookies and some mixes for when we want to bake."

She took her dishes to the sink and raided the pantry for cookies. "You got my favorite." She held up a bag of shortbread sandwich cookies.

Sven followed her with his own plate. "Those are everyone's favorite. Now go relax and save us some."

The recliner was every bit as comfy as the bed. She popped the footrest up and curled her feet underneath her and tore the bag open. The first four cookies might have been the best thing she'd eaten all week if not for that dinner. The next two cookies were pretty good and the two after that were just okay. She rolled the bag closed and left it on the coffee table separating the recliner and couch from the fireplace and television.

The view of the kitchen was even better than the cookies. Both men had their backs to her as they washed and dried the dishes. Her inexplicable non-attraction to Sven from their fake picnic date had disappeared and her libido was confused, swirling between admiring Sven's shoulders and ogling Carlos's butt. No, that wasn't the part of her that was confused. Her libido was just back to its normal, healthy, active state. Either the months of taking care of herself had made her hungrier for the real thing, or attraction to these particular guys had grown with exposure.

A jaw-splitting yawn caught her by surprise. For a day that started with an undercover mission where her fire power was outed to the public and full disclosure was announced to the world and ended hiding in a remote forest, it was surprising she was still awake. She checked the time on the television receiver. It hadn't been eighteen hours since the shower orgasm, but waiting until morning would take her over that limit.

She swung the footrest down and untangled her legs. "I'm going to change and stretch out for a bit. The cookies are here. Save me some for later, please."

They acknowledged her with waves and nods, though she thought Sven looked a bit too knowing about what else she'd be doing in her room.

The bedroom doors were solid and heavy but without locks. However the cabin was heated, it either wasn't on or hadn't reached the bedroom yet. She pulled a loose t-shirt and lounge pants from her bag and stripped off her clothes. With a selection of vibrators packed, she selected a neon green torpedo-shaped one with a very quiet motor.

Leaving the clean clothes on top of the bed, she slid under the covers and closed her eyes. She called up the anonymous hands she imagined stroking her body and she slid one hand over her breasts and the other guided the vibrator between her legs. Her imagination sent the pair of imaginary hands over her breasts, paying special attention to her nipples. Another pair of hands slid down her sides and cupped her ass. She hadn't meant to make another set of hands. After a moment of surprise, she forced her body to relax and enjoy the doubled sensations.

Strokes with the vibrator matched the rhythm of the hands. Anonymous hands. Anonymous hands that came with flashes of warm brown eyes, dimpled smiles, and welcoming laughs. She pushed those visions away and focused on the rhythm deep within until the buildup burst in a wave of pleasure.

Her head sank into the pillow as she relaxed into the afterglow. Where was her mind? The last time was a one-off of letting her imagination assign identity to her anonymous imaginary hands. Fantasizing about real men, men she knew, was always off-limits. Another of her rules, along with not dating men she worked with. Thinking about breaking one rule led to breaking the other, maybe? Damn subconscious brain. And two men? How was she supposed to choose?

Two telepathic men.

That fact muddied how her subconscious was choosing attractions.

Confrontation? No, not really. But she had to ask, had to know for herself. She slid out from under the blankets and into the shirt and lounge pants. The vibrator had to be stored. She gave it a quick wipe-down with a towel and into its bag where it would be out of sight if anyone glanced into her room.

The other bedroom's door stood open and it was dark inside. In the living room, the guys were side-by-side on the couch with the cookie bag between them. Sven was munching while Carlos studied a pamphlet.

Iona plopped into the recliner with a sigh. "Can I ask you a question?"

Sven swallowed his cookie. "You me or you him?"

She chuckled. "Both of you."

"Sure." Carlos set the pamphlet in his lap. From her vantage, it looked like instructions for the entertainment system.

Her hands were unsure of where to go. She pulled one foot up and wrapped them around her knee. "I don't mean to accuse, but I need to know, for my own peace of mind, were either of you in my head just now?"

Sven shook his head emphatically. "No. We wouldn't."

"Well," Carlos said slowly as Sven shot him a look. "We're never in your head, but we keep our minds open just enough to hear you in case you call for us. It's the same level we listen whenever we're on duty. Is that okay?"

She nodded. That meant it was all her. She dropped her forehead against her knee. "Yeah, that's fine."

"Everything okay?" Concern colored Sven's voice.

She blew out a breath. "I'm just going through some stuff and trying to figure out where it's coming from." She leaned back into the chair in time to see a look pass between the men.

Sven cleared his throat. "Is there anything we can do to help?"

"Do you need us to get you in touch with Doc Choi?" Carlos added.

She laugh-snorted. "Let's leave her out of this." They were both watching her, so she added, "It's a bit personal."

Sven coughed. "About the you-know-what you had to tell me about?"

Carlos looked from Sven to Iona with a look of utter confusion.

She asked them rapid-fire, "You don't know? You didn't tell him?"

Sven shook his head. "Not my place to share your business."

"Thank you." She stared up at the ceiling and counted her breaths for several moments. "You really should know, since we're exiled out here together." She made eye contact with Carlos first, then with Sven. To tell him, she couldn't maintain the contact so she studied the view outside the window. The paired porch lights illuminated circles that reflected off the railings and the front of the car.

"So, over the years, it's become clear that the more I use the fire, the worse my control gets. After any intense session, strong emotions make it just burst out. I don't know how much you've heard about why I've been in the infirmary."

Carlos cocked his head to one side. Adorable, but it looked like he was out of the loop as far as bureau gossip went. Sven gave her a slight shake of his head and her heart melted. She hadn't expected him to protect her secrets so fully.

"When I got home from the last forest fire job, I was with my boyfriend and things got heated." She winced at the unintended choice of words. "Damn. He got third-degree burns over most of his back. Bureau docs fixed him up, but he's a normal so they wiped his memory. He doesn't remember me at all. They set me up with Doc

Choi to figure out a cure, best case, or maintenance at least."

Carlos blew out a soft breath that whistled through his lips. "I'm sorry. How long were you together?"

"Only a couple of months and some of that I was out of town. I thought we were getting to the point of talking about making it serious." She blinked back unexpected water from her eyes. "Anyway, lots of trial and error. The doc found a brain trigger that diffused the build-up of whatever but it needs electrodes in my head. Some sedatives keep the fire under control, but I can't use it when I'm on them. The best solution so far is regular orgasms. Every eighteen hours for now, but we're still testing." Even though she was looking out the window instead of at them, it was hard to say it aloud. "It could be so much worse, but embarrassment isn't likely to kill me. Or anyone around me."

Carlos leaned over and patted her leg. "Let us know if there's anything we can do to help."

"Thanks." She closed her eyes again. "I'm just trying to figure out where my head's at. Or whatever's doing the thinking for me. And figure out what to do about being attracted to both of you."

Sven snorted. "That's an easy one. You're not attracted to me. Those kisses at the reservoir did not come from a woman who liked me."

"And I couldn't figure out what was wrong with me that I didn't. You're all the things I normally like in a man, but I was still broken. Constant exposure to you might have cured me. But—" She turned her smile on Carlos. "Carlos is just as amazing. You're both wonderful and perfectly sexy and I don't—"

A knock against the door made her jump enough to ram her knee into her lip. She jumped to her feet. "I'd better get it in case Dupree came back."

She pulled the door open as Sven said, "It's not."

Cube stood in the circles of light on the porch. Heat grew in her palms. She raised her palms and let a flame bloom in each. "How did you find us?"

Cube stepped back, raising his hands in impotent protection. "The Movement had trackers and telepaths, too. The Bureau watched us, we watched you."

She grew the flames higher, the heat warming her face. "Had?"

He backed another two steps, still within the porch light's glow. "Wait, wait. I come in peace."

"Hear him out. Lower the fire." The voice was Carlos's, but she felt Sven's presence in her mind as well, both calming and reassuring.

She pushed the flames down, but kept her palms up. At her back, the men's solid presence backed her up, warm and strong. "What does the Movement want with us?"

Cube's mouth curved into a gentle smile. "The Movement is over. We accomplished our goal today so we don't need to exist anymore." He stepped closer. "I used their resources to find you, but I'm here on my own."

Iona called the fire close to the surface, but kept it from flaming. "What else do you want with me? You've done your best to make me a target."

He spread his hands wide and low. "It sucks that they called you out. They shouldn't have done that to anyone. It's not the Movement you're hiding from, it's the normals."

"Because the Movement made me a target."

"I know. I wish they hadn't. We knew full disclosure would rattle the normals, but I hoped they'd focus their fear and anger against the government. Instead, they've made you a target."

"Still doesn't explain why you're here."

Cube took two tentative steps towards her. "Full disclosure means more opportunities for all of us."

Carlos rested one hand on Iona's hip. Warm and supportive. Firefighting, she was used to the rest of the team having her back, but this was for her, keeping her emotionally safe as well as physically safe. "Full disclosure isn't announced yet. All we have is Movement amps on film at one event."

A smile spread across Cube's face. "One event filmed by several news networks and spread all over the world in under an hour. You might not have heard about the press conference yet."

She wasn't going to give him the satisfaction. "And you're sure it's not to explain away what they saw?"

"I hope not. It's already been titled 'New Information on Amp Genetics and Abilities'. Sounds like the first steps to full disclosure to me."

"Fine. What if it is?" A light wind blew through the trees, for early summer, it was chilly here in the woods. She let the fire flow just beneath her skin, warming her. Sven stepped closer. Either he wanted to share her heat, or he was being protective. She hoped it was the first.

"If it is, I'm going into business. Setting up a job-finding service for amps. Starting with heat—and cold—controlling amps for now, but maybe adding electricity and magnetism manipulators later." His gaze flicked past her at the men. "Sorry, I'm not planning on including mentals, but somebody will."

Well, he'd done his homework. "We already have jobs."

Cube reached into a pocket and slowly drew out a card. "For now. Here's my card in case you want to make a change. Feel free to share it with anyone else you know."

Iona stayed on the porch. Cube slowly approached, the card in one outstretched hand. When he was at arm's length, she reached out and plucked the card from his fingers. "That's it? You drove all this way just to pitch a job?"

"I was on my way out of town anyway. Might as well head to the coast and go south from there. New Mexico and Arizona have some places really interested in people who can freeze food for storage. I'm guessing Palm Springs will as well." He stepped back and sketched a wave. "I hope I hear from you, but if I don't, best of luck to you."

The darkness swallowed Cube as he turned and walked away from the cabin. They waited until they heard a car door click closed and an engine start out on the road.

Sven smacked his fist against the door jamb. "That greedy SOB. Everything's turned upside-down and he's hoping to make a profit. We could blow his engine from here, but then we'd be stuck with him."

"Yeah." Iona extinguished the latent fire completely and rubbed her suddenly cold arms. "Back inside?"

Sven locked the door. "I reported him to the office. Lucent's said the Movement's headquarters house is empty and up for sale already."

Iona slumped against the end of the couch. "So they planned ahead. They knew they'd get disclosure out. Someone's tracking them all, right? That stunt still broke a few laws, and the ringleaders can be arrested for conspiracy."

"Sounds like the team is continuing to track them all." Carlos relaxed his stance, but stayed close enough for comfort. "Our report on Cube already has them alerting teams along the coast highway and down south."

"Good." Iona turned to face them both. "I don't want to be angry the rest of the night." She took and released a deep breath. "Before we were interrupted, we were talking about me figuring out who I like and how much. Ok if I test that out?"

They both made agreeable sounds. She reached for Sven's face first and pressed her lips against his. The kiss grew from deep within her and built, heat—but not flames—rising under her skin. She probed his lips gently with her tongue and wound her fingers through his hair. It wasn't a kiss that she could hold forever, something would break.

Regretfully, she pulled away, her lips the last part of her body to lose contact with his.

He moaned. "That was nothing like the kisses at the reservoir."

"That's why I'm trying to figure myself out." She looked into Carlos's eyes. "Your turn. Okay?"

He held her gaze and nodded mutely.

She wondered briefly if they were telepathing about this. Wondered and decided it didn't matter to her. It was what they did.

With a single finger, she stroked his cheek. Carlos leaned into her touch. When his eyelids lowered halfway, she pressed her lips against his. They were soft and warm and parted slightly. She increased her pressure and his arm slipped around her waist, holding her in place. Iona took that as a good sign and deepened the kiss, running her tongue along his lips.

A moan escaped from deep in his throat.

Sven laughed, breaking the mood. "I think that means he likes it."

Iona broke off the kiss and rested her forehead against Carlos's. Then socked Sven in the arm. "He didn't interrupt your kiss."

Carlos's cheeks were flushed and his eyes downcast. Iona raised his chin with a finger, their foreheads still touching. He met her gaze and she pressed a kiss to the tip of his nose. "Thank you." She stepped back. "Both of you. I still don't know what's going on with me, but it's going on with me and both of you. Okay if I go to bed now? I need to sleep on this. And I'm really tired."

They each placed a hand on her nearest shoulder. Carlos cleared his throat. "You've had a really long day."

"Yeah," Sven added. "We'll lock up out here and put the cookies away. Sweet dreams."

"What other kind would I have knowing you're both here?" She intended to sound lightly flirtatious, but it came out overtly sexual. She ducked past them both and headed down the hall with an attempted-at-cheerful "Goodnight".

They answered in kind – Sven's with delighted mischief in his voice, Carlos's with wistful longing.

She closed her door as softly as possible and slipped under the covers, burying her head and hoping she hadn't just messed everything up.

"Hey." Sven nudged Carlos to distract him from whatever caused that blank look in his eyes. "I'll lock the door, you can get the cookies."

"Sure." Carlos looked down the hallway to the bedrooms.

"You okay?"

"Maybe." Carlos rolled up the open top of the cookie bag and carried it to the kitchen.

Sven followed and leaned his elbows on the counter. *"Do we need to talk about that?"*

Carlos blew out a deep breath. *"It's just... I've never had a kiss like that... ever."*

"You haven't kissed all that many people."

Carlos shrugged.

It was true. Sven could count on one hand, with fingers left over, the number of serious girlfriends in Carlos's past. *"But I agree, both kisses were spectacular."*

Carlos pushed the cookie bag to the back of the counter and lean-sat on the edge. *"Do better kisses mean stronger feelings?"*

Sven's turn to shrug. *"Sometimes. Or it just means they're better at kissing. Hard to tell. But there were strong emotions behind these ones. On both sides. All three sides."*

"A triangle."

"Not unless we close the third side." Sven stood and took two steps to close the distance between them. *"Want to try?"*

Carlos looked up, his deep brown eyes looking directly into Sven's soul. *"You and me? I didn't think blonds were my type."* But he tilted his face up until their lips met.

A wave of emotion rocked through Sven as they kissed. The warm hominess of comfort, the sweet tang of love, the heat of attraction. He worked his jaw carefully, drawing Carlos deeper into the kiss. Carlos matched his intensity with eager pressure back against Sven's lips.

Carlos eased away sooner than Sven wanted, but he released the kiss.

"Wow," Carlos said barely louder than a whisper. "Seems like we might have tried this sooner. Does it mean we're bi?"

Sven chuckled, the sound low in his throat. "It might. Or it might mean we only like kissing people we're emotionally connected to."

"I always knew that about me. I just never thought about you in this way. Except for the mental connection, it was as good as kiss as Iona's." Carlos rubbed his cheek. "But you have more stubble."

Sven rubbed his chin. "I promise to shave before we try again."

"It's a deal." Carlos stretched up on his tiptoes and kissed Sven's stubbled cheek. "But now I need to get to bed."

"I'll shower first, but I can find my bed in the dark. I'll try not to wake you."

"A cold shower?" Carlos suggested as he eased around Sven.

"We'll see."

It wasn't a cold shower – he'd never believed in denying himself when other options were available. The shower stall was the right size to lean against one wall and let the water pound against his body. A tight fit for more than one person inside though. Too bad. With a steam fogging the shower door and the memory of those kisses, Sven brought himself to a shuddering conclusion.

He didn't shy away from thinking about her and Carlos while he pleasured himself. Thinking about how he might help them to their satisfaction heightened his sensations.

Tomorrow was going to be interesting.

CHAPTER ELEVEN

As long as she ignored the sliver of sunlight through the gap in the curtains, Iona could pretend it was still night time.

A tappa-tap-tap on her door spelled the end of that idea.

"Hey sleepyhead. The disclosure briefing is about to start." Sven sounded entirely too cheery and awake already.

She flung the blankets off and pulled on fuzzy socks. The briefing could be world-changing for all amps, she shouldn't miss it. She stopped in the bathroom to pee, brush her teeth, and check her hair. The dark color startled her, almost having forgotten she'd dyed over the red.

The walk from bathroom to living room was far too short. Last night's kisses still burned on her lips and she hungered for more. Coming between two best friends was so high on the 'don't do it' list. Both had been pushing her towards the other. Did that mean that neither really wanted her?

She squared her shoulders and lengthened the last two strides into the room.

Sven had the recliner and half waved a greeting. She settled on the couch with Carlos who handed her a mug of coffee. "There's breakfast too. I thought you'd want to watch this first."

This, so far, was a morning news program with a scrolling line below imploring viewers to remain for the upcoming press conference on the latest news on Amplified Human abilities. "Do we know who's speaking yet?"

"Hasn't been announced, but Cast said it's the Bureau head." Carlos sipped his coffee.

Iona sniffed her mug and met Carlos's eyes over the rim.

He shrugged. "There's hazelnut mocha creamer in it. I hope you like it."

She took a cautious sip and gave him a smile to show her approval. "It's good. I'm just used to black coffee first thing, and fun flavors later."

"I'll get it right tomorrow," he promised.

Sven regarded them both. "We'll have plenty of time to get things right."

She sighed. "Yeah. Vacation on the Bureau's dime. At least I don't have a pet to worry about."

"Us either." Sven sipped his coffee. Probably also hazelnut mocha. "But Carlos always wanted either a little dog or a lizard." He gestured to the television with his mug and tapped the remoted with the other hand. "It's starting."

They watched in near silence as first the White House Press Secretary talked about how vital amp citizens were to the Bureau's mission and for national security before introducing the Chief of the Bureau. An amp herself, she spoke for twenty minutes. Talking about how amps now had more abilities than just speed and strength and that Bureau scientists and doctors were continuing to study them while still maintaining the privacy of citizens. She only gave the briefest description of these 'new' abilities but included all the classes – mental, sensory, manipulation, and pheno.

Interestingly, she did explain that pheno amps had different outward appearances as their other ability and gave examples of those with fur, tails, or oddly-textured skin.

She emphasized, repeatedly, that the Bureau's mission hadn't changed. They were still there to assist law enforcement where amp abilities would help, and to step in when crimes were committed by amps. Another mention of citizenship came with a thanks to all those who came to America from other countries to become citizens and add their strength to ours.

Sven and Carlos both smiled at that and high-fived across the space between the chair and couch without looking at their hands. They interlocked their fingers as their palms met and they left them clasped for several moments before they slid slowly apart.

The Press Secretary stepped back to the podium after the Chief finished and took questions from reporters. He answered some himself and directed others to the Chief. Nothing new was revealed in any of their answers and the briefing wrapped up after another fifteen minutes. Immediately after, a program with its regular panel of political experts opened with a discussion of the announcement.

Sven muted the panel. "Well, it's about what we suspected might happen."

Iona swirled the remains of her coffee. "It's still a lie. Just about our parents and grandparents, not about us."

Carlos chuckled. "Anyone else count how many times she said 'citizen'?"

Sven clicked the television off. "At least every third sentence. Good point about our parents. The bureau has records of all the amps that have registered, but not the personal details. Someone should suggest that as many as possible write down their stories. Once full disclosure is adjusted historically, we'll want those stories."

Iona's mum had talked a little about how she first realized her powers, but nothing from her grandparents. "There's some published already, but they only go as far as speed and strength. We can start posting to bureau message boards, and talk about having the first generation record how things were for them. They'll have to stay private for now."

"For now," Carlos murmured. "Did you catch just how they covered their bases? When they're ready to reveal that we've had the powers all along and that the government knew, they can either cite personal privacy and national security, or say that it was the decision of a previous administration and the new one wants to be fully open with the American people."

Iona shook her head. "Unless that administration hates this one, or us. We can hope for the best. Either of you still talking to Cast? Does this briefing affect our vacation here?"

"I'll ask," Sven said. "There's some breakfast things on the counter. We didn't know what you liked best."

Carlos stood. "And while you eat, I can show you what I found outside."

She followed him the few steps to the kitchen. 'Breakfast things' turned out to be a loaf of bread, a bag of bagels, butter, cream cheese, bacon, sausage, and a carton of eggs.

He opened one cupboard door. "Plates are here, silverware in the top drawer."

"Toast is enough. It's close enough to lunch time anyway."

He bundled everything else away while she popped two slices into the toaster.

"Do you ever toast them by hand?"

"When I was a teenager and still trying everything out. Marshmallows were fun. Sticky, but fun. The toaster toasts more evenly." She leaned against the counter where she could see several trees out the window, but not much else. "So you went exploring this morning?"

He leaned against the counter opposite. "Yeah. Filled the gas tank and checked out the store. It's got milk, eggs, bread, and snacks, but when we run out of anything else, we'll have to head down to the towns along the coast."

"Doesn't sound like something you can show me from here." She took a gulp of the cooling coffee. "This is good. Thanks."

"That's one of our favorites." He turned to look out the window with the trees. "I looked around outside when I got back and found the hot tub Sven was hoping for."

The toaster popped and Iona pulled the slices out and coated them with butter. "In the back?"

He nodded towards the corner behind the table where they'd eaten the night before. "That's a glass door behind the curtain. It leads to a cute little patio with the tub off to the side. It's not really hot right now, but we should be able to find the controls and get it warm enough.

Iona had a slice of toast in one hand so she had to put the coffee down to hold out her palm and call up a tiny flame. "Heating it won't be a problem."

He grinned. "You are so cool. Um, I guess I mean hot?" His grin stayed, but color bloomed on his cheeks. He pointed out the window to a spot alongside the back of the cabin. "Anyway, if you don't have anything appropriate to wear, we can take turns in it once it's hot enough."

She extinguished the flame and finished the slice. "No worries. I packed a swimsuit."

Sven must've heard. "You keep a swimsuit in your go bag?"

"You were planning on skinny-dipping?"

He shrugged. "If I have to. I have some boxers that work."

It was hard to tell if that dimpled smile was a flirt, or a joke. Carlos was the easier to read. At least his blushing made him seem interested. If only she could talk to Lisa about it, but hiding out up here meant that her telepathic roommates were her only means of reaching her.

Would choosing one of them hurt the other? That's what it all came down to. Right now, she thought she could come to love either of them. If it hurt the other one or ruined their friendship, she'd rather keep searching for Mister Right-for-as-long-as-it-lasts.

"So," Sven said. "Are we planning a post-breakfast pre-lunch soak?"

Carlos arched one eyebrow. "Weren't you checking with work?"

"Yeah, that. No change. Probably know more in two weeks. They've had five interview requests this morning for Flame. On top of all the ones from yesterday. National's going to identify some agents with less-threatening powers to show off first. Sense and some phenos, I think. If that goes well, they'll release some records of cases where other agents used their powers 'for the good of the nation'. Maybe even authorize a television show about them." Sven watched their faces. "Now can we check out the hot tub?"

Iona set her mug on the counter. "He said it's not warm enough yet. If you find the controls, take the cover off, and make sure it's been cleaned recently, I'll come warm it up."

She went to her room as noises from the kitchen sounded like the men went outside. Lisa would be a nice safe choice for the Bureau to publicize. The power of super-smelling, able to track lost hikers and missing toddlers. She'd also hate being publicly identified.

Hopefully, they'll choose someone who would enjoy the attention. Iona pulled her shirt off and tossed it on the bed. Neither of the guys mentioned last night's kiss. Either they were being respectful and taking it slow, or they wanted to forget she'd done it. Sometimes she envied their ability to read emotions.

Her suit was simple – one piece, blue, with high cut legs and a plunging back. It showed off her legs satisfactorily. She plucked at the front of the suit. Her breasts didn't fill out the front at all. *It's not like they don't already know I'm lacking in that department.* She hesitated over her t-shirt and grabbed a clean towel to wrap around her waist instead.

Outside, they had the cover off. Sven stood beside the log-framed tub tugging his jeans down past his knees. His striped red boxers clung to his butt, and they were still dry.

Carlos fiddled with a box on the wall under a wooden awning. "I'm ready to make the bubbles once you like the temperature."

Sven stuck a finger in. "Still cool. Can you make it 102?"

"Precisely?" Iona tried to arch one eyebrow at him. She failed, but had never managed it before.

"Close?" he pleaded, making an attempt at puppy dog eyes. That was more successful than her eyebrow lift.

Carlos joined them at the edge of the water. "I set the thermostat for 102, but it'll take a while on its own." He still wore his jeans and t-shirt.

Iona swirled one hand through the water. It was just under body temperature. She sent heat, but not flame, radiating out from her palm and kept swirling. She dipped her other hand in periodically to test the temperature and checked the half-logs surrounding the tub to make sure they weren't getting too hot.

Sven swung up onto the deck surrounding the side of the tub opposite the house and rested his feet on the steps, putting his knees level with her eyes. "Is it working?"

"Almost there. Go ahead and check."

He leaned over and checked the water. "Nice. Just about perfect." He swung his legs around and dangled his feet in the tub. Now the side of his well-formed butt was at her eye level.

She sent another burst of heat, carefully aiming it away from his feet. "Okay, you can turn on the jets now."

Carlos did something and bubbles whooshed forth, sending the water surface roiling.

Sven flicked his fingers at her, a sprinkling of droplets splattered across her face. "Get in before I use up all the bubbles." He looked past her to Carlos. "You, too."

"I know how to make more," Carlos said. Iona climber the four steps to the tub-side deck and pulled the towel off. Carlos followed her, removing his own shirt and tossing it beside the towel on the handrail.

Iona caught her breath. For some stupid reason, she'd expected Sven to have a nice body, but hadn't guessed Carlos would look as nice. Both were remarkably fit for amps whose talents were using their brains, literally, instead of their bodies. Not a full six-pack, but flat bellies and a light dusting of hair over a lightly muscled chest.

Sven splashed her again, more water this time. "Get in and give him room. That deck isn't that big."

She scooted in and sat across from Sven, facing the cabin. She could just see Carlos removing his jeans without turning her head. The hot water could explain any redness on her face. His swim trunk-clad butt was every bit as glorious as Sven's.

She stretched her legs across the floor of the tub. "You said you have the same birthday, who's older?"

"Me," Carlos said.

"By two minutes." Sven sent a tiny splash towards him. He looked down and nudged Iona's foot with his own. "What's your foot doing over here?"

Ulp. She snatched her foot back. "Just looking for a water jet to massage my foot."

Sven held his hands out. "Give it here. I'll do a better job."

She didn't want to read too much into the offer, but he seemed genuine about it and she lifted the foot up to his hands. Within moments, it was clear that he didn't exaggerate. Strong thumbs stroked up the sole of her foot, kneading the muscles without tickling. She closed her eyes and sunk down to let the water cover her shoulders and she could rest her neck back against the rim of the tub.

A moan of pleasure escaped her throat before she could stop it.

Sven chuckled. "There's more where this came from."

He released her foot and she squeaked in frustration.

He laughed out loud. "Hand me the other one. What did you think I meant?"

"You don't have to answer him," Carlos advised. "It'll only make his jokes worse."

She kept her mouth shut along with her eyes, the better to enjoy his ministrations. He stroked each toe and finished with a feather-light caress. Her foot was lonely without his hands on it, but she pulled it back and rested it on the floor of the tub.

"Any other talents I should know about?"

He stared over her head, then nodded decisively. "Back up singing. I'm great at it."

"That's a pretty specific talent."

Carlos snorted.

"And it only works with him." Sven grinned and started singing, just sounds with a doo-wop beat.

At the fifth repetition, Carlos added the melody. She recognized the song by the second line. "Uptown Girl". The sly looks from Sven made her wonder if they'd chosen the song for any particular reason. After a verse, they switched over to "Why Do Fools Fall in Love". Sven's backup part barely changed, but he continued with enthusiasm.

Carlos appeared to be concentrating on his singing, not looking at her, but off at something past her shoulder – a tree maybe. Sven kept darting looks at her and adding back-up-dancer style arm movements that threatened to smack Carlos or send sheets of water across the tub.

When they changed songs to "Silly Love Songs", she was sure they were directing this impromptu concert at her. Though during the last few choruses of "I love you", they tilted their heads together adorably and gazed into each other's eyes.

Just asking how they felt about her was the mature thing to do. She handled dangerous tasks all the time. This shouldn't be that hard.

She applauded when they let the last words trail off into silence, splashing herself in the face as they bowed their noses to the water's surface.

"Are you sure you can't influence emotions?"

Carlos shook his head. "Nope."

Sven wiped water from his nose. "Maybe you're just good at reading or receiving emotions? Or we're just that good at song."

"That must be it. Your singing." They really were good, though Sven's exuberance and charisma overshadowed Carlos's presentation.

Sven cleared his throat. "Or those kisses are still haunting you."

Haunting. Embarrassing. Hungry for more. "Are you saying I kiss like a ghost?"

"If ghosts kiss like that I need to spend more time in haunted houses."

Carlos's cheeks glowed red under his golden-brown skin.

"What have you done when you like the same woman or when a woman likes both of you?" Her question seemed to surprise them. Sven arched back, showing off his pectorals nicely.

Carlos threw his head back, then glanced at Sven. "It's never happened before. I can't think of anyone."

"Carley M back in second grade?" Sven suggested.

Carlos shook his head. "She pretended to like me to get to know you better."

"I'm sorry that happened so often. It wasn't fair to you."

Carlos nodded, then grinned. "Not Maria. She hated you." He looked at Iona. "Maria called him 'El Gringo'."

"What happened with her?"

"We were all nearly done with college. Sven and I were going to apply to the bureau. She wasn't an amp and didn't understand why he and I were so close. She never gave me an actual ultimatum but it was her or him… and she knew I'd pick him and the bureau. Haven't heard from her since."

"That sucks."

Sven shook his head. "It was my fault and I didn't even know it then. Most of his breakups probably were my fault."

"And plenty of yours were mine," Carlos said.

Iona looked from one to the other. Trying not to linger her gaze on their lips. Trying and failing. "You're both single because you haven't found someone who'll put up with your family?"

Carlos nudged Sven. "To be fair, I haven't been looking very hard. I'm not into picking someone up in a bar or at a party. I'd rather get to know them first and see if a relationship develops."

Sven unfolded an arm and laid it along the edge of the tub behind Carlos's shoulders. "I've tried meeting women at parties or bars plenty of times. None of them lasted more than a night or two. Part of it's the job."

Carlos sighed and leaned back. "I do miss kissing. You reminded me how much."

Sven tapped his far shoulder. "You her, or you me?"

Iona leaned towards them. This was new information. Maybe her liking both of them was moot.

Carlos exhaled loudly. "I meant Iona. But yours was nice too."

"We should have tried that years ago," Sven waved his free hand dramatically. "All that time we missed out."

Iona pressed back into the tub's bench. "Does that mean you're done looking for women?"

They looked at each other. Sven gave Carlos a quick peck on the lips and grinned at Iona. "Nope. Just now we know we have options."

"Well, now I don't know whether to kiss you or not."

Carlos looked down at the water. "I vote yes."

"Me, too." Sven sounded more enthusiastic than Carlos.

"Why do you get a vote?"

"I like watching kissing. And maybe I'll get one later."

She studied his mouth. "Maybe."

He rubbed his chin. "We both shaved and everything."

She slid across the tub, aiming for the space between the men. "Considerate of you."

The men shared a look and a giggle that she knew referred to their kiss. How had they gone their whole lives without considering it before? Too wrapped up in the idea of heterosexuality, probably. At least their semi-hetero natures were to her benefit. She reached up to stroke Carlos's cheek and ran her wet fingers back through his hair, slicking it back from his face.

"It feels perfect to me." She touched her lips gently against his. He melted into her touch, pressing the kiss deeper. She slid the tip of her tongue just up against his lips and withdrew it. When she repeated the movement, he parted his lips just enough. Her heart thumped loudly, the sound filling her ears and the throbbing delving further down her body with each beat. He slid a hand along her waist and rested it just above her hip bone. Nothing more. Just resting. No demanding or pulling.

She left the hand that stroked his cheek resting on the lip of the tub, not ready to trust the fire just yet. With the back of her other hand against his arm, she stroked the length from his hand at her hip up to his shoulder and put that hand on the tub's edge.

A soft moan escaped Carlos's mouth. She wanted to stroke his arm again. Or his back, but didn't dare. Not yet. Instead, she sucked at his lower lip.

He ran a hand along her shoulder. No, he couldn't have. One hand on her hip. Her other hand was beside his shoulder and would have felt it move. Sven must be tired of waiting. His fingers played along the top of her shoulder and stroked the side of her neck. Kisses followed the same path as his fingers.

Then she felt Carlos move his other arm. He stroked it up her side and along her arm and over to Sven. She opened her eyes just enough to see whether he was pushing him away or drawing him in. Opening them wasn't needed. Carlos pulled Sven closer, sandwiching her between them. Not trapping her – neither of them had a hand or leg behind her. If she'd wanted to leave the delights of this intimacy, nothing was stopping her.

The freedom made the kisses sweeter. When Sven's kisses along her neck neared her earlobe, she pulled back by millimeters from Carlos and turned her head to Sven. Sven's kiss was more experienced, more confident and adventurous. His tongue reached out before hers did.

Between the hot water and the heat these two were creating inside her, she couldn't tell whether her fire was behaving itself. She broke off the most excellent kiss and pulled his hands back from the edge of the tub.

"Before we go any farther, I need to you both promise that if you feel my hands getting hot, you'll get away as fast as you can. No exceptions."

Sven shrugged. "Sure. You've been keeping to your schedule, so it shouldn't be a problem."

"Untested waters." The water lapped against the bare skin above her swimsuit. "Pun not intended."

"I promise." Carlos stroked her knee, not going any higher.

His knee was within easy reach. She stroked it while turning her lips back to Sven. Slowly, she swirled and traced her fingers higher up his thigh until they teased at the edge of his shorts. Eventually, he took the hint and ran his own fingers higher up her leg. It only took a slight outward twist of her knee to guide his fingers to the inside of her thigh. He grazed a particularly sweet spot and she moaned against Sven's mouth.

Was she moving too fast? She hadn't really known them until recently, and only flirting for this past week or so. Sven wouldn't feel rushed, but Carlos didn't give off the same vibe. She trailed her fingers higher up his leg and he didn't stop her. Making sure her hand stayed outside his shorts, she brushed the back of her hand against his bulge.

He moved into the contact and she let her hand return to the spot randomly in its explorations.

Sven moved his mouth back from hers just far enough to speak. "What are you doing to him?"

"I'd show you, but I'd have to move." She resumed the kiss as he made a noise that sounded like assent.

It didn't take much untangling to flip over so she was straddling Carlos's lap.

A soft, "Oh my," was his breathless reaction.

She leaned into his welcoming lips and let one hand drift over to Sven's leg where she trailed it higher up his thigh until she could show him what she'd been doing while kissing him. Sven helpfully scooted closer. Then nibbled along her shoulder to her neck.

When he reached her earlobe, he sucked it gently before whispering. "We might want to move this inside so we can keep going."

She drew out the kiss she was sharing with Carlos then moved the kisses around his jawline to his ear. "Do you agree with him?"

"Let's go."

She leaned away from his body, leaving her mouth on his as their last point of contact above her hips. He trailed a hand from her shoulder down her arm as she slid backwards off his lap. As soon as she was mid-tub, Sven stroked Carlos's cheek and kissed him every bit as deeply as either had kissed her. Blond hair against dark, light skin against brown, palm against cheek, lips against lips.

"You know how hot that is, right?"

Sven looked over his shoulder at her. "Hot from this side, too." He ran his fingers through Carlos's hair, wetting the side Iona had left dry. "I'll put the cover back on. Meet me inside."

The morning air wasn't warm enough to stand around wet so she hurried inside. By the time she had towels ready for them both—nice thick navy terrycloth—the guys were latching down the tub's cover. Carlos stayed to help instead of following her inside.

Together, they made a perfect couple. No matter whether they were a couple of friends, brothers, or lovers, they were still perfect together. *Sigh.* She couldn't do anything to mess that up. She'd never forgive herself. Maybe this, whatever this was, would be a mistake.

She started to sit on the couch, paused to remember the wet suit under the towel and hovered awkwardly between couch and recliner. When the guys entered, Sven's arm around Carlos's waist, and both laughing, she was still standing and fiddling with the edge of her towel. They joined her, wrapping their free arms about her waist.

"I didn't sit because I'd get the couch wet." She tried waving one hand towards the still-dry seating instead of leaning into their embrace.

"What's wrong?" Carlos asked, his mouth comfortably just below her ear.

She sank against them. "This, us, you. Am I making a mistake?"

Sven nuzzled her hair. "You haven't done anything yet."

"But I need to mention my dating track record isn't great."

"Pffft. You didn't date amps before."

"Mostly."

"And you haven't dated us."

"You haven't been an 'us' very long."

One hand—Carlos's—rubbed her lower back. "We'll learn together."

"Promise me I won't mess up what you two have."

"It's not possible." Sven sounded sure.

"You've never fought?"

"A little." Sven released her from the hug and Carlos a moment after. "But when you feel each other's emotions, you can't hurt the other person. Not if you have any empathy at all. What if we agree to try it out while we're here? Then, before we leave, decide if it's worth continuing once we're back in the real world."

"I'm willing," Carlos, reaching for her hand, "but only if we're all in agreement."

She accepted his hand and rubbed her thumb against it. "Okay. As long as you promise to tell me if I'm doing anything to come between you. I'm attracted to you both, I like you both, and never want to hurt either of you."

Sven took her other hand. "It's a promise."

"I promise too." Carlos squeezed her hand.

"Okay." Her towel slipped and she grabbed at it. "I need to get dry clothes first."

"The way we were headed, I don't think clothes are necessary," Sven said with a wink.

Carlos shoved his shoulder against him. "How about we start out clothed? Dry ones though."

Sven nodded. "Okay. Change and meet back out here?"

"My bed's big enough for all of us. Better than the couch."

"Meet in there, then?" Carlos looked from her to Sven. "I don't sense anyone outside who might interrupt."

No interruptions were a good thing. The few steps to her room didn't allow much time for thought. Her brain was liable to make up enough reasons of its own. If she'd only stop thinking about all the ways she could mess this up, this could work. At least this 'trapped in a cabin away from the rest of society' trial run of a relationship. Relationship was a loaded word.

She peeled off her suit and hung it over the room's only chair. There wasn't time to plan the perfect outfit, and that would be trying too hard. Not that she'd packed for a romantic rendezvous. Yoga pants and a loose t-shirt with a pattern of constellations – easy to put on, easy to take off if/when necessary.

One of them tapped on her door, so she perched on the foot of the bed. "Come in."

Both were similarly casual, Cargo shorts and a black t-shirt for Carlos and wildly patterned blue and green board shorts and bare chest for Sven. She let herself admire that physique during the three steps they needed to cross her room. Lightly muscled and liberally dusted with blond hair, he was just as nice to look at bare as he was clothed.

They both sat, one on either side of her.

Carlos took her hand. "Where do we start?"

Kissing him felt right. So she did. He responded eagerly, and gratefully. Maybe they couldn't affect other people's emotions, but Iona refused to believe that they didn't sometimes project their own emotions.

Sven rubbed her back, slow circles from her waist up to her neck. She relaxed into his touch as she leaned into Carlos's kiss. The warmth from both mixed together and met in a delightful swirl that flowed down to settle near her heart. When Sven's lips took the place of his hand, that warm swirl moved lower.

She slid her free hand across Sven's lap, up his chest to his opposite shoulder, and down his arm to find his other hand. Moving slowly, she leaned back until her back was flat on the bed. Sven's kisses moved from the back of her neck to the side, and then along her collarbone. Carlos's kisses stayed on her lips, but his free hand stroked down her side to the top of her thigh.

She released their hands and coordinated stroking both their chests, up and down, lightly scratch over the nipples, up and down again. Carlos gasped against her mouth and she teased his lips with her tongue. Pulling back just enough to speak, she whispered, "How far do you want to take this today?"

His hand froze on her hipbone. "I'm willing to go as far as you want. Did anyone bring condoms?"

Sven's mouth stopped it's teasing route over her shirt towards her breast. "It's like you don't even know me. Back pocket."

Iona ran her hand from his chest around to his back and down over the elastic waist of his shorts. There was a pocket and there was something inside. Sliding her hand inside, she cupped his butt and grabbed the packets with two fingers and drew them out.

She handed both to Carlos. "Keep these where we can find them when we need them." While he scooted up to put them on the bedside table, she drew her legs up onto the bed and pushed up to the center.

Sven snuggled against her side, his free arm across her belly with fingers splayed out and his other hand stretched with those fingers curling through her hair. Carlos propped himself up on one elbow and trailed the other hand down her arm to interlace their fingers. She guided those fingers to her breast and released them, freeing her hand to curl around his head and pull his lips close enough to kiss.

That made it more kisses for Carlos than for Sven. Did it matter? Two sets of lips, of hands, of other more intimate regions. It felt like she should be keeping track to make sure she paid equal attention to both of their parts. Sven's hand trailed up to the breast she hadn't guided Carlos towards. The delightful sensations of fingers deftly swirling around in seemingly random spirals to tease her nipples through the soft cotton of her shirt made Carlos's kisses even more urgent. She gulped them, savored them, arched her body into all the contact.

The thin shirt was suddenly too much in the way. She reluctantly pulled back from the kiss. "Give me a moment to get this off. You two carry on without me."

She wriggled down away from the kisses and out from under those talented fingers. By the time she had her shirt off and tossed to a corner of the room, Carlos and Sven were kissing and carefully running fingers across each other's chests and hips.

"Still hot." She placed a hand on the uppermost knee on either side of the space she'd so recently vacated – now very much narrower – and stroked upwards until she cupped those beautifully formed butts and watched the kissing. Watching was almost as good as the actual kissing. Almost. Mostly, it made her want more.

Throats were available. She wriggled up and kissed her way from Sven's earlobe down to his broad chest and Carlos's fingers there. A deep purr from at least one of them encouraged her. She licked her way around a conveniently placed nipple, then drew a long finger into her mouth to suck and tease with her tongue.

Someone stroked her hair, then reached her jaw and tilted her head up to join the kiss. Sven's lips first, then Carlos's. She swirled her fingers through the blond hairs across Sven's chest, then ran fingers along Carlos's t-shirt collar. "You have us at a disadvantage. This needs to come off."

Sven chuckled, the vibrations rumbling through his chest. "She's right. Off with it."

Carlos disengaged, and Sven took the opportunity to monopolize Iona's lips. His kisses were expert and experienced, but no less sweet. His tongue prodded her lips apart as Carlos returned, shirtless, to her side.

Soft, tiny kisses pressed against her breast and she rolled onto her back to reach both men. Carlos captured her nipple with his lips and sucked, his tongue flicking against the tip. She gasped against Sven's mouth and arched her back to achieve fuller contact.

Both of her hands were free. Lying on her back between them, she could run the backs of her hands against the crotch on either side. A moan from Carlos and pressing into her hand from Sven rewarded her touch.

Emboldened, she stroked more deliberately, rolling her knuckles along the stiffening bulges on either side.

"Shit." Sven broke off his kissing and rolled away from her contact.

It didn't seem like she'd done anything wrong, but she snatched her hand back.

"Dammit Cast." Carlos scooted away leaving her breast bereft of his mouth.

But at least that explained it. 'No interruptions' indeed. Telepathic disadvantages.

They were out of reach, so she cupped her own breast and ran a thumb over the breast that hadn't just been lavished with kisses… Sven met her eye, dropped his gaze to her hand, and shut his eyes tightly. Her pants were just going to be in the way when they returned to her sides, so she slid out of them and tossed them after her shirt. Their inattention must have only lasted moments, but time stalled for those moments and she ached for their return.

Finally, Sven opened his eyes and took her hand. He pressed a kissed against it. "I'm sorry, but Cast is the last person I want to think about when I'm with you."

"God, yes," Carlos added.

"Anything I need to know about?" She regretted asking immediately. Official reports were not her priority right now.

"Not really. We're still ordered to lay low up here, keep you out of the public eye. They're putting media spots together, but it'll be at least another week or three."

She willed her smile to spread slowly and seductively. "You mean we have no time to waste. Get those shorts off." The men were still both half sitting so she reached a hand behind each head and drew them back down to the bed's surface.

"Mmmm, where was I?" Sven asked, stretching out his fully naked length against her side.

Carlos cupped her breast on his side. "You were about to hand me those condoms."

"Of course I was." Sven leaned over to retrieve them and kissed Iona while passing them over.

She dragged one fingernail down his chest and pulled her lips away long enough to ask if Carlos wanted help.

"It's under control."

She returned to the kissing, but reached down to cup Carlos's balls while he dealt with the condom. Instead of putting it on, he reached across her belly, angling his elbow so it teased her nipple and rolling the side of his hand over her mound. Sven gasped and moaned against her mouth. She kept teasing Carlos's balls with one hand and reached for Sven with the other. Carlos was already there, stroking along Sven's shaft with the condom between his knuckles. Room enough for her hand to slide past and cup Sven's balls. He released her mouth to moan when she dragged her fingernails gently along the soft skin.

Carlos slid up to take Sven's place at her lips. She played her fingers along his bare shaft with one hand while keeping the other on Sven.

Sven nuzzled her breast and someone tapped their fingers against her clit. Then she lost track of who was where. One or the other of them was sucking a breast, licking her clit, kissing her lips, or stroking somewhere along her body. She kept a hand on each of them, running her fingers through one's hair while stroking the other's cock. At some point, Carlos added his condom so she couldn't immediately tell by feel which one she had in hand.

She arched her back and lifted her hips into their contact, whimpering with need.

One pushed into her as the other sucked her breast. Someone rubbed her clit. They matched their tempos – tongue and fingers and cock, switching places whenever she approached climax. After the second time, it was clear they planned it and she whimpered her displeasure.

"You two and your telepathy. Enough with the teasing." She wrapped her legs around the most pertinent hips—Carlos's as it turned out—and kept him in place until she came to a gasping, shuddering conclusion.

They kissed her, then kissed each other. While they were occupied, she wrapped her hand around Sven's sheathed hardness and gave it a series of rhythmic squeezes. "Give me a minute to recover, then we can take care of this."

"I can help if you need me to," Carlos said, wrapping his hand over hers. "It might take both of us."

Sven ducked down to her neck. "I'm right here." He bit along the curve of her throat.

"Oh, like you two weren't telepathing about me the whole time."

Carlos flipped Sven over onto his back. "Not just about you. Some of it was about us."

"Hold him there for me." Overcoming the lassitude keeping her prone, Iona rolled up on top of Sven. Carlos slid across Sven's chest and stopped whatever comment Sven was about to make with a deep, deep kiss.

Iona rocked her hips faster and faster until Sven bucked and cried out. She flopped down, sandwiching Carlos in the middle. "I don't know about you two, but I could get used to this."

Sven untangled an arm and stroked her cheek. "I'm just grateful that we sorted this out already. Can you imagine going a week or more here still thinking you liked the other one best?"

She nodded and kissed his palm. "Or worrying that liking either of you could ruin your partnership."

Carlos gave them each a quick kiss. "I'd say this relationship experiment is off to an excellent start."

The reminder that this was a test to see if a trio could work for them sobered Iona instantly. They must have read it in her face—or telepaths, duh—because Carlos was quick to add, "By the end of a week, we'll know each other's favorite foods and colors and how best to annoy you."

"And," Sven added with a wriggle of his hips, "All our favorite sex positions. Though this one will be up there. You're gorgeous when you're on top of me."

"Nothing's hotter than watching you two kiss."

Sven captured her hand and pressed it to his jawline. "I'm going to have to keep shaving this close, aren't I?"

It wasn't sandpapery yet. But he'd just shaved a few hours ago. "It's nice and soft like this, but let it grow for three or four days and it'll be soft then too."

"Just be careful how you kiss for those days," Carlos warned. "My skin is too delicate for stubble-burn."

Sven rolled onto his side, toppling them both off. "Stubble-burn is not on my list of turn-ons. Time to get cleaned up and explore our temporary home. Ladies first in the bathroom."

Her first impressions were accurate. Kind, respectful, hot. Glad her brain and body were able to agree about that. A week would be too short a time here, but the uncertainty about her new-found 'fame' was a cloud hanging over the cabin.

CHAPTER TWELVE

After a month of their idyll—Carlos called it a honeymoon and Iona had no reason to suggest he call it anything else—they had a comfortable routine. Wake up, usually tangled in the same bed; morning sex; breakfast; hike or jog through the woods; soak in the hot tub; lunch; read, play games, or do puzzles; dinner; another walk outside; evening sex.

It was the most relaxing time she'd ever experienced. She tested her control over her fire daily, sometimes more than once a day, and her confidence grew with every day she maintained perfect accuracy.

She hummed about the kitchen with the contentment of morning afterglow while Sven and Carlos showered. Two just barely fit in the cabin's shower, if you were willing to be very close – but not all three of them. She radiated heat from both palms to make toast, adding just a touch of flame for a crispy finish.

When the pipe squeak told her the shower was turned off, she heated a pan—on the stove, not with her fire—and got the last of the eggs from the fridge.

"There's news," Sven called from the hallway. He came into the kitchen shirtless, still toweling his hair.

"Real news this time?" Iona cracked an egg and let it drop to the pan. "Or just more of the same?"

"Time to go home. They've called us in. The last three or four—Cast wasn't that specific—public opinion surveys have the normals mostly happy about us among them. Having Lisa, Gator, Morrison, and others from other cities doing the talk show circuit just made them all popular. There is a movie and a TV series in production about amps and Hollywood is trying to hire lots of phenos and manipulators as special effects actors. Viral videos are making the rounds – some of ours and many that we left alone. No one's asking about the fire-starter with the red hair anymore."

Carlos joined them – he'd taken the time to get a shirt, but not to button it. "And they'd like us back tonight, ready for assignments tomorrow."

She waved one hand towards the now-sizzling egg. "We can eat breakfast first, right?"

"We're not that far away." Carlos passed Sven with a pat on that nice firm butt and peered into her pan. "And we need more eggs than that."

She kissed his cheek. "I was interrupted. Go butter the toast while I crack open the rest of these. He can check the fridge and sort for eat, toss, or pack."

Sven shook his head. "'He' will pack up the bedroom and ask what we need to do about the bedding. There's not room at the fridge right now." He sauntered back to the bedrooms.

Once she got all the eggs into the pan, Iona figured out how to ask her question. "Did they say whether I was reporting back to the infirmary tonight or on my own?"

"It was Cast, he probably doesn't have that information. You can call from my place and ask. They didn't save your last place did they?"

She stirred the eggs. They were ending up scrambled whether she wanted them that way or not. "The Bureau put all my stuff in storage. I'll have to find a new place if Doc Choi signs me off."

"Our building has two other units. Maybe one will open up. It's all Bureau amps." He smiled, the warmth brightening his eyes. "Or, we each have a two-bedroom apartment, the two on the second floor. If we rearrange some stuff, you could move in with us."

That was the question she hadn't figured out how to ask. "You both want to continue this experiment of ours? You think it'll work back in the real world?"

He set down the plates he'd picked up and placed a hand on each of her shoulders. "We love you, you love us, and we love each other. The Bureau encourages inter-office relationships. If we can work out where to put the furniture, we're all set."

"You make it sound pretty simple. Your mom will be okay with it?"

"She'll love you. She's used to him being part of my life, so that won't be a huge surprise. Now, stir those eggs so I can use the pan for bacon after I butter the toast."

"All right slowpokes," Sven called from the hallway. "Our go-bags are packed. If we hurry, there might be time for one more soak in that tub." He leaned on the counter and stared longingly outside.

"Sorry, lover." Carlos hip-checked the still-shirtless Sven. "We need to eat, clean up our mess in here and get on the road."

Iona ran a hand over Sven's chest. "And you'll need a shirt so he can keep his eyes on the road."

He kissed her then, deep and hungry. "I kept a shirt out."

She returned the kiss with enthusiasm. "What do you think about his suggestion? You want me to stick around?"

He wrapped both arms around her and whispered in her ear. "I love it. I can't imagine not staying together." He leaned back without releasing her. "If Doc Choi releases you right away, we'll make space for you and sort out furniture later. If it takes her a few days, we're start rearranging enough to at least give you closet space and a room of your own."

"You two are amazing. You almost make me regret not dating Bureau guys for so long."

Carlos joined the embrace. "I'm glad you waited for us. If you found someone else at the Bureau, you wouldn't have given us a second look."

She cupped his butt. "I can't imagine anyone not giving you a second look. Breakfast is getting cold. Can we continue this love-fest later?"

Their final cabin breakfast was over too soon. Carlos sent Iona and Sven to load the car and take a final walk through the forest while he cleaned and packed the kitchen.

Loading the car took only one trip. Sven took her hand and led her around the back so he could gaze longingly at the covered hot tub. "If we ever decide we've outgrown the apartments, let's get a place where we have one of these."

She leaned into him, hugging his arm. Had she ever had a boyfriend who talked about their future? This month with the two of them was longer than most of her relationships lasted. Three more months and she'd set a new personal record. "I'd like that. Maybe in the hills, with lots of trees like these?"

"Perfect." He pressed a kiss to her temple. "I love that you aren't questioning your control any more. A vacation was good for you."

"The company had something to do with it. Let's ask for time off together next year." 'Next year', now who was planning for the future?

"Done. Carlos agrees, so I just asked the telepath on duty to log it in the system."

Neither of them were put off at all about the idea of a future together. Instead of saying something about it, Iona just squeezed his hand.

They rounded the cabin just as Carlos came out the front door. "All set in here. Housekeepers will be here tomorrow to take the laundry. Take one last look for anything and we can head out."

The back seat of the car felt safer – even with the assurances from the office that no one was asking after the red-haired firestarter anymore. Plus, sitting in the center, she could see both of them in three-quarters profile.

"Goodbye little cabin in the woods," Carlos said as he pulled the car out of the winding drive onto the forested road.

"Goodbye tiny town with no useful stores," he said as they passed through the gas station intersection.

"Goodbye little road that's not on all the maps," he said as they pulled onto the narrow highway leading back to the city.

"Are you going to do that the whole way home?" Sven asked.

"I think it's sweet," Iona said.

"All done now," Carlos promised. "Those were the places I passed the most getting groceries and gas. Now settle in for a nice quiet drive home."

Home. One they'd invited her to join. As much as anything else, this made her feel welcomed into the team they'd formed. She slipped off her shoes and pulled her legs up onto the seat. The forest outside flashed by and gave her an alternate view to the handsome men before her.

"Is that smoke?" Sven shook her out of her mindless musing.

A thin trail of dark smoke rose from a car pulled off the road ahead.

"Too dark for steam," Iona confirmed. "Pull over, but stay way back."

Her eyes never left the little green hatchback. As Carlos brought his car to a stop, Iona was already opening the door. "Check on the driver and contact someone in the office in case we need to call 911." Before she set foot on the ground, a flame shot up from the car's hood. Wind blew it sideways, away from the road, but towards the too-close forest.

She hopped barefoot across the graveled shoulder to the grassy verge, both hands held palm out in case it was needed. Sven raced to the car and knocked on the window. He grabbed the door handle and pulled. It took him a couple of tries, but it opened. Before Iona could see what happened to the driver, a gust of wind caught the flame and blew a trail of sparks onto the thin strip of grass.

A week without rain meant the grass was dry enough to catch fire. Iona ran up the slope, avoiding rocks, brambles, and bits of branches to stay uphill from the fire. A tiny flame burst to life a foot from the edge of the gravel. Iona sped up; within a few steps there was a circle of burning grass ten feet across.

Five more strides and she reached out her hands and sent a burst of flame to char the grass surrounding the fire. From the edge of the road, uphill to the top of that circle, then she ran around it and burned grass clear on the far side.

The fire she'd created obeyed her will. She pushed it into the center where the natural fire flared bright. Her fire surrounded and consumed the natural fire, binding it in a tight ball in the center of the blackened area. With a sharp twist of her wrist she extinguished all the fire. Dark smoke still poured from the car's hood. Carlos had a fire extinguisher in hand and white powder covered the car and surrounding gravel.

A cheer from the road reminded her there were witnesses. All those years of having to hide her skills flooded her with panic until she realized the cheers were from Carlos. After one final glance at the burn for lingering sparks, she picked her way down to the road.

"Wait up," Sven called, running up the slope to her. "You really need to wear shoes up here." He scooped her up in his arms and carried her. "Everyone's fine. The driver is in shock, he was scared for his granddaughter asleep in the back seat. We got them out and help is on the way."

His arms were warm and strong under her back and knees. The lingering smell of smoke coated them both.

"How much did they see?"

"He was fussing over his granddaughter and trying to call for a ride home, so wasn't paying attention. She woke up as soon as we opened her door and filmed the whole thing. I asked her to send me a link when she posts it."

She buried her face against his neck. "This new world is going to take some getting used to."

He kissed her hair. "If it's any consolation, her phone camera is older and probably couldn't capture your face at that distance. Watch yourself. I'll set you on the car."

Carlos bounced up to her. "That was amazing! How do you feel?"

"Hungry." She held out one palm. "But look – total control." She willed a tiny flame into existence and spiraled it around her hand before extinguishing it in a puff of sparks. "This vacation, and both of you, are very good for me."

"Whoa! Can you do it again?" a small voice asked.

Carlos intercepted the little dark-haired girl. "No, niña, she needs to rest now."

She cocked her head to one side. "You sound like Abuelo. Can I ask her for an autograph?"

Autograph? That was new. Iona nodded. "Sure. I don't have anything to write with."

The girl whipped open the small purse hanging from her shoulder and pulled out a purple pen and notebook. Iona opened the book to a blank page and wrote 'Flame' with a squiggly flourish beneath it. She returned the pen and held the page carefully with one hand and scorched the edge of that page with the other.

The girl's eyes grew wide. "Cool!"

Iona fanned the book to make sure no heat remained and handed it back.

"Thank you! My name's Juanita Maria and my abuelo is Alejandro Torres. I've never seen an amp before and none of these new powers you have."

"Juanita. That's enough time to thank our heroes." The grandpa approached and placed one hand on the girl's shoulder. "Thank you so much for stopping the fire from spreading and getting us out of the car. I'm glad we have heroes like you to help the rest of us."

A distant siren startled Iona. "Is that for us?"

Sven squeezed her hand. "For them. Fire department and a tow truck are on the way. Alejandro called his son to pick them up. We can go as soon as the first of them get here."

"Okay." Iona hopped down from the car. Gravel bit into her bare feet. Carlos opened the back door and Sven lifted her again and deposited her inside.

"Cheese, jerky, and chocolate are in the bag behind my seat." Carlos pointed. "Start on those and I'll get something to drink from the cooler."

By the time she'd dug up the snacks—protein and carbs—the firetruck had parked nose-to-nose with the disabled car and firefighters in full gear were examining the car and the burned grass. Sven was talking to one of them with lots of accompanying hand gestures. Juanita and her abuelo were talking to another, Juanita bouncing from foot to foot.

Sven rejoined them, all wide smile and dimples. "We're cleared to go. They have our bureau contact information and are very pleased with your work here. If you ever want to leave the Bureau, any fire department in the state would hire you."

As the guys settled into the car, Iona leaned her elbows on their seatbacks and looked from one to the other. "I'm right where I belong."

ABOUT THE AUTHOR

When not writing, Jill Webb reads, takes care of her horses, and works in micro-electronics. She lives in Oregon with assorted horses, dogs, and cats. The cats only interfere with the writing a little bit.

Acknowledgements

I would like to thank the editors and cover artist at SinCyr Publishing for all their dedicated work getting this book (and those for other authors!) published. Sienna Saint-Cyr has a wonderful vision for the company, Rhiannon Rhys-Jones is brilliant at spotting continuity errors and keeping details straight. Lee Moyer is a wonderful artist who helps me bring my characters more fully to life.

Thanks also to my weekly writing group – BJ, Cameron, Ashley, and Che – for pointing out where I've left story details in my brain instead of getting them on the page. And thanks to beta readers and friends who've encouraged me along the way: Kelli, Anya, Tammy, and the writers I've met through Cascade Writers.

CPSIA information can be obtained
at www.ICGtesting.com
Printed in the USA
LVHW031202160321
681669LV00010B/367